A LOVE FOR MIA

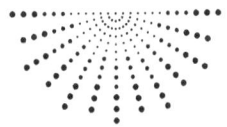

L. OSBORNE

This book is dedicated to all the black women all of the world. We make the world go round. Stand up and be great!

L.Osborne

SYNOPSIS

A love for Mia

Mia has stood by Giavonni through years of infidelity, holding onto a love that continually tested her limits. Giavonni crossed an unimaginable lines and when Mia finds out it sends her world as she knew it into a tailspin,

Mia's loyalty was finally stretched to its breaking point. The betrayal leaves her torn, but the final blow comes unexpectedly, ripping her open in ways she never anticipated.

Realizing this was costing her too much, after nearly losing her life , she found herself finally letting go, and stepping away from a love that left her hollow.

In the midst of her recovery, someone unexpected

enters her life—a friend who begins to show her what it means to be cherished and loved with respect. As he becomes her safe place, Mia finds strength and healing in his presence, even as the shadows of her past try to pull her back. With newfound clarity, she embraces a future where she's free to love and be loved in a way that honors her worth.

TRIGGER WARNINGS

Trigger Warnings:

• **Domestic Abuse:** This book contains depictions of domestic abuse, which may be distressing to some readers.

• **Mental Abuse:** Scenes of mental abuse are present and could be triggering for individuals sensitive to psychological manipulation or emotional harm.

• **Child Loss:** The book addresses themes of child loss, which might be upsetting for those who have experienced similar events.

• **Stillbirth:** There are descriptions of stillbirth, which may be difficult for some readers to process.

• **Murder:** The narrative includes acts of murder that are detailed and intense.

• **Murder-Suicide:** Themes of murder-suicide are

explored within the storyline, potentially triggering for some audiences.

- **Suicide:** The book contains references to suicide, which may be distressing for individuals affected by similar experiences.

These trigger warnings aim to provide readers with the information they need to make informed decisions about whether to engage with the content. If you need further assistance, feel free to ask!

PROLOGUE

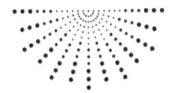

*M*arch 2014

I press send on my phone, and immediately, the hate in my belly begins to subside. The deed is done, and now I only have to sit back and wait for the chaos to ensue.

"If only that bitch had realized who she was fucking with I wouldn't have had to do this," I say to myself as I get up from my bar. I put my phone on DND and pour another glass of wine as I curl up next to my future husband on the couch. I hear G's phone start to vibrate and snuggle closer to him, knowing that he's not going to get the phone while I have all this ass this close to him. He picks up the phone and turns it off before placing it on the table.

"Take these off," G says tugging at my shorts.

I ease my hips up and allow him to pull my boy shorts down my legs. He spreads my legs and begins to kiss up my thighs. The feel of his lips on my skin ignites me. I begin to tremble from the intense heat that builds in my core. Just as he reaches my inner thigh, he lies down, pulling me up closer until I'm sitting on his face. I gasp as his lips fold around my center. My slickness on his face makes me want to explode. My screams grow louder as the pressure of my release builds in my apex. As I hear G moan while devouring my soul, I reach back and grab his swollen dick and begin to stroke him through his shorts, his precum making a damp spot on the front. The closer I get to releasing on his face, the faster I stroke his dick.

He begins to pump my fist and moan. My desire to taste him postpones my release. I flip over so now I am face-to-face with the girth and length my throat has grown accustomed to. I take him into my mouth, and his arms fold around my waist holding his meal in place. The cool breath that he blows on my sensitive clit makes me take all of him in my mouth.

His lips part as he groans when I devour him with one suck. He pushes into my mouth to the hilt, and I begin to use my tongue as he eases out of my mouth to lick up the vein pulsing from pleasure.

"Fuck, baby, take all this dick," he groans, and I suck him back in.

I use my tongue and throat to milk his dick while covering his moans with my sex. As I moan on his dick, he licks faster, building that pressure again. My sucks begin to match the rhythm of his. I hum while his dick is in my throat, knowing that this is his kryptonite. The vibrations in my throat tease him while I continue to suck and massage his balls that have now migrated up to prepare for release just as mine becomes imminent.

Finish him.

Using my hands to stroke him faster, I focus my mouth work on the tip. As the suction falls in rhythm with the strokes, I hear him call my name, and I take all of him in my mouth as we cum in unison. I grow light-headed from the release, but I am satisfied.

I wake up to the sound of Giavonni arguing with his mother. Is she here? In my house? What the fuck is she thinking coming here?

"Let me tell that bitch what I really think about her gold-digging ass," I hear Janet scream.

I know she's not talking about me like that. When I get up off the couch, I hear him say to her, "Ma, you need to leave. And I told you to stop talking about my fiancé like that."

She smacks him. "Who do you think you're talking to like that? Can't be me. I'm the reason you have all this shit, including your funky ass little dick that you be letting these little whores suck on."

When she says this, I stop to hear his response.

"Ma, don't start that mess. I need this to work out with Mia. I really want to be with her."

Jane scoffs at his words. "You're so damn dumb you don't even know the reasons that you're supposed to get married. You can't even look me in the eye and say you love her. And before you try, remember where the hell you were last Wednesday and Thursday night."

I think back to when Giavonni said he had to go out of town for press after he signed his contract. I had believed him, but his mother's words insinuate something else. When I look back, this is the first seed of doubt planted in our relationship.

The next day, I waited until after breakfast to ask him where he had really been, but instead of answering me, he told me that I had no business texting his mother last night when she just wanted to know where he was.

I pull out my phone, unlocking it and going to the message thread until I land on the video that his mother sent last night. I slid the phone across the counter until it hit him in the arm.

"Alexa, turn up the volume." The sound of two people fucking starts to play in the kitchen, causing him to look down at what's playing. When the video stops, he looks at me in shock. "This is what your mama sent me last night after she left here. Maybe you should scroll up and read where she told me I'm a useless slut that has probably slept around and won't be able to give you a baby."

He moves around the counter to hold me, but I don't want him anywhere near me.

"Fuck you and that piece of fat shit mother of yours. I'm leaving. Don't look for me. I can't imagine being with someone who could fuck a bitch in his mama house, and to add insult to injury, your mama decides to record it and send it to me. You both deserve each other. Oh, and the next time that you want to defend me, maybe you should tell her about sophomore year and who really sacrificed so that her precious baby got into the NFL."

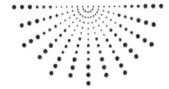

CHAPTER ONE

"*D*id you fuck him, Mia?"

The anger in my husband's face is evident and it pisses me off more. After all the women he's been with over the years, he really has the audacity to question me? The fucking nerve. In this moment, I wish I was guilty of whatever he's trying to gaslight me into believing is my fault this time.

"HELL, NO G!" I scream at him as tears spring from my eyes. "Are you really trying to accuse me of some shit because you think I am finally getting my lick back?"

The venom in my voice assures him that the tears that escape my eyes are the anger trying to escape my body and save his life.

"Kimber!" He says, like this tricks name holds any

validity in this scenario. "She sent me a message on IG saying that you met up with Sincere when you went on that little girl's trip and fucked her husband." The disgust in his voice makes me even more mad. How can this man judge anyone when he's a public playground at this point?

"She's lying, and unlike your cheating ass, I can prove it!" I say as I dial Sincere's number, making sure that the phone is on speaker so that I can watch the stupidity wash the anger from G's face.

"What's up gorgeous?" Sincere says, sounding like his usual self.

"Hey Sincere, I need your help clearing something up for me," I answer, hoping G realizes that if I wanted this man, I could have easily had him. "Why does your wife think that we fucked when I saw you in Vegas last month?"

My tone is even, and I watch the tension build in G's biceps as he crosses his arms.

"Is this a fucking joke, Mia? That shit not funny!" I can hear him shifting gears in his car, so I know it's safe to continue.

"No, Sincere, I'm dead serious. Kimber wrote Giavonni, saying that we fucked," I say in an annoyed voice.

"Shit! Yo, I'm sorry that this shit is happening. She has been acting strange lately, accusing me of shit and swearing that I am sticking anything that moves. She's been calling every female in my shit." The exasperation in his voice rings through with truth.

"Well, that's unfortunate, and I absolutely hate that for you, but you really need to get your shit together, Sincere. I told you that she's going to burn everything around you if you don't get a handle on this shit. She's playing with fire, and you know better than anyone that I will bring gasoline and watch her world burn!" I say in a harsher tone then intended.

"I know, Mia. Shit, what you think I'm trying to do? I love the girl, but she's fucking crazy. Yo, tell G I'm sorry for this shit and that he knows I would never disrespect your union like that." He says it with the sincerest tone.

I reassure him that we are okay before disconnecting the call.

I turn to face G, thinking that I proved my point, but the look on his face lets me know that he may not be as convinced as I think. He turns to leave the house, grabbing his keys from the key rack.

I raced across the kitchen behind him. "You just heard him apologize for this, so why are you still treating me like I've done something wrong?" The rage grows as I walk to where he originally stood.

"How the fuck did you get that nigga number to call him, and why the fuck didn't you tell me that you saw him while you were in Vegas?" The weight of his words knocks the wind out of me.

This nigga can't be serious. "So, you really are fucking crazy huh? First, you accuse me of fucking the man, so I prove you wrong. Then, you turn around and find another reason to be pissed off? Typical G. That's just fucking typical of you." I scream as he slams the door before peeling out of the driveway.

"Fucking Asshole!" I scream at nobody as he leaves me alone. Again.

"GIRLLL, I told you something is not right about how G has been acting. He would have never come at you like this a year ago. Now suddenly, he acts like you a thot out here in these streets," Maya says with more annoyance in her voice than anything.

"I just don't know what to do about this whole situation. He was cool with me having Sincere as a friend, and now he's acting crazy like he didn't know that I have the man's number." I stretch out in my bed and move my phone to the nightstand so that I can get all the snacks off the bed.

"I keep telling you if you want me to find out what he is doing, I will find out faster than a cat can lick his ass." We burst out laughing in unison at her old lady sayings.

"You are so damn crazy. Let me get off here so I can shower and get some sleep. I hope wherever he decided to lay his head tonight he stays there because I'm sick of this shit." In the past, these words used to haunt me, but tonight I say it out loud to start healing from the hurt that I'm sure is on the cusp of coming to the light.

I wake up hours later and realize that G is still not in the bed. I roll over and pull my phone from the nightstand. It's 2:22 am. I open the BMW app on my phone to track his car. It's parked in an unfamiliar residential area. Scrolling on my phone, I pull up the Maps application and paste the location and notice that it will only take me thirty minutes to get there if I leave now. Closing the phone, I stop and stare at the ceiling and wonder if I'm prepared for what I might find. What if I pull up and he has a whole ass family there? I wait for the tears that used to come, but they never do, so I close my eyes and try my hardest to drift back off to sleep.

"WAKE UP, BEAUTIFUL! IT'S TIME TO BE GREAT!" My alarm blares the affirmation in my ear.

"Would you turn that damn thing off?" G says from behind me.

His voice startles me when I realize that he's actually in the room. "Oh, you found your way home I see."

Getting up, I turn my alarm off and sit up on the

side of the bed to face him. "Why are you here? If you don't want to be here anymore, why do you keep coming home?" My voice comes out in a tone that is unfamiliar to me.

It's unfamiliar to him too, because his eyes pop open, and fear glints in them. "I went to my homeboy house to chill for a little while and try to cool off." The defensiveness in his tone mixes with the uncertainty. Watching him squirm gives me all the information I need about what he was doing last night. Getting up from the bed, I toss back over my shoulder, "Bet!" knowing he wouldn't know how to take my tone.

CHAPTER TWO

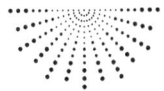

"*B*itch, you have the patience of Job!" Maya says as I tell her about what transpired before I left home.

"I don't think you're supposed to curse and reference the Bible in the same breath, My," I say chuckling.

"Whatever, girl. I'm just saying that I would have waited for him to take a shower and whipped his ass like Regina King did in *This Christmas*."

We both burst out laughing as we shout in unison, "WHY DON'T YOU STEP OUT OF THE SHOWER SO WE CAN TALK ABOUT IT?!"

Our laughter is interrupted by an incoming call from G. "Speak of the devil," I start.

"And he will show his ugly face!" Maya finishes.

"Hold on, girl, and don't hang up!" I say.

"Girl, put it on conference. I will mute my phone," Maya quips.

"Alright, but make sure you mute, heaux!"

"Thank you for calling the sexiest woman in America. How can I help you?" I answer, trying to sound as normal as possible, knowing that I just added Maya into the conversation.

"Hey, mama, can we talk?" he asks with hesitation.

I can tell from his tone he has something pressing to say. "Talk quick, I'm heading into this meeting. What's up?" My tone sounds more urgent than loving.

"Babe, I just want you to know that I love you, and last night I just needed to wrap my mind around everything going on. We have been in such a strained place since my accident, and I don't know what to do to fix this."

Bzz bzz. I look down at the text message that Maya sent from the other side.

> MyMy: Suggest counseling and see what he says.

Her message is a great suggestion since we both know that he has refused to go year after year. "Well, maybe we should really try counseling so that we can learn to better communicate and just figure out what is going on with us." My tone is calm and genuine because

I want us to go to counseling so somebody else can let him know he is not always right.

He shocks me when he says, "Normally, I would be against the thought, but I feel like we can both benefit from it."

My mouth falls open, and I almost drop my damn Caramel Frappuccino with extra caramel drizzle all over my white pants. I was ready for the reluctant reply that he always gives. Never in a million years did I think that he would be willing to go to counseling, let alone with me. Especially after he was hell bent on me being the issue.

"Okay then. We can research counselors together," I reply.

"Nah, you find the person and I'll show up. I trust your judgement, bae." By the way he's handling this, I'm sure he isn't taking this seriously, and this is just another tactic to get me to stay.

"Alright, well I need to go now. I'm about to be late. We can talk more about this later in the week."

I hear him smile as he says, "I love you, Mia."

I check my phone to make sure that the call has been disconnected with him before I give the all clear to Maya. "Alright, we are good, Maya."

Her laughter comes over the line abruptly, and it causes me to start laughing. "Bitch, you must have him scared by not arguing with him this morning. We both know that fool thinks nobody knows better than him. And you didn't even say I love you too." Her cackles echo through the phone.

Before I can respond, my reminder chimes in letting me know that my meeting really does start in twenty minutes. "My, I need to go, girl. I have a meeting today with Sincere's organization about the budget for the fundraiser."

Sincere and I decided to work together on the project for my charity in the local community called Young Black Men of The Future.

Maya gasps and says, "Biiitcccchhhhhh, you still going to work with his organization? I mean, I'm all for it, but I have never seen you choose violence."

Rolling my eyes, I reply, "This is business, and you know damn well I am all about my bag and supporting my boys. Jealous wife be damned!"

Through spurts of laughter, Maya says, "Jealous G, too. But alright, girl. Love ya, bye."

I disconnect the call, thinking that maybe she is on to something. Is G going to be upset about this? I quickly push the thought to the back of my mind as I pull up and allow the valet to open my door. I grab the ticket and smile as I glance down to see my favorite number, four hundred forty-four, in big bold numbers. I say a quick prayer before I enter the building to ensure that I am in the headspace to handle the business in front of me. "Be with me ancestors, help me bring this home!"

I cross the lobby after checking in with Daniel at the desk security. He points me in the direction of the conference room we would utilize for our scheduled meeting. I'm in awe at the inside of the building. The all-white marble flooring with the leather seating in the waiting area gives way to a beautiful crystal chandelier. The conference room is just on the other side of the chandelier with two large glass doors that open into the most elegant conference space I have ever seen. The oak wood table has a centerpiece of red and gold leaf marbling. In the center of the table sits two dozen white and two dozen purple roses.

The sight of the roses makes me stop and flash to a conversation that I had with Sincere when we were little.

"One day, I'm going to make millions of dollars, and whenever I close a deal, I will have white and purple roses on the table," I said to Sincere all those years ago as I swung at our deserted school.

"Why do they have to be white and purple roses?" he asked, looking confused.

"Because white roses are for purity, and I will enter into an agreement with a pure heart and mind. And purple because it's my favorite color, but it's also a symbol for adoration," I exclaimed in my youthful exuberance.

"Well, one day, I just want to make millions so I can spend it on anything but stupid flowers," he said, laughing at me.

Jolted back into reality, I hear Lesley's voice coming down the hall and turn just in time to greet her and her assistant.

CHAPTER THREE

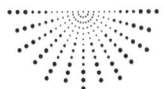

*a*s I sit in the conference room, I find it hard to listen to the proposal from Sincere's partner, Lesley. I find myself trying to understand just what went wrong yesterday and thinking if I even want to be with G anymore. I'm pulled back into the conference room by the delectable smell of someone entering the room accompanied by an unfamiliar heat that settles over my body.

I glance around the room to see if I can pinpoint the direction of the heat burning into me. When I look up, Sincere quickly looks away.

"So, what do you think, Mia? Do you feel like the small changes are doable to make this partnership work for the fundraiser?" Lesley asks with a big smile on her face. I can tell that she's excited about the ideas that she presented me with for the project. But if I'm honest, I haven't heard a word she said since the beginning of this meeting.

Thanks for fucking my mind up once again, Giavonni!

He always throws me off my square on days when I have important shit to do. Mix in Sincere walking in the room and smelling like heaven, and I didn't hear anything. Thank God I had already looked at the proposal before this meeting and came prepared to sign today. "I think everything looks great, Les," I say rising from my seat to shake her hand.

Sincere walks over to where we're standing, and I feel the slightest thump in my panties. After years of just being friends, this is the first time that it's ever happened to me. The realization of it all makes my skin flush.

"Can I see you in my office please, Mia?" Sincere asks, causing everyone to stop as if they are just now realizing that he's here.

"Sure Mr. Cummins, as soon as I sign these documents with Les."

I hope he doesn't hear the lust washing over me as I turn back to Lesley. "We can sign in my office," he says as he picks up the contract off the table and holds his hand out for me to proceed in front of him.

Sincere is the CEO and founder of Cummins Consulting Company. He started the company after moving back to the city after he buried his father. His father always wanted him to come back and run a nonprofit but that had never been his passion, so I was shocked when his partner Lesley reached out to me regarding my organization. We had been running in the same circles but hadn't crossed paths professionally since he'd been home.

As I walk in front of him, I realize that I have no clue where I'm going. "Do you want to tell me which way I should be going?" I ask as I turn to find him smirking. I look up at him as he towers over my 5'4" frame.

"This way," he says, grabbing my hand and leading me in the direction that we were originally walking in.

"You could have just told me that I was going in the right direction," I say, giggling. What the hell am I doing? Am I really flirting with a man that I have known all my life? I literally just cursed G's trifling ass out for accusing me of the very feelings that I'm having. But maybe G was on to something, because the way that I feel right now makes me want to see just how deep—.

"Would you like something to drink?" Sincere says, letting go of my hand.

The second his hand leaves mine, it leaves a void. It's weird, here I am having these feelings that I have never had for this man, and I can say I have never had for any other man besides G, and I can't explain them. What the hell is going on with me?

Focus Mia, I think as I try to remember why Sincere stands there staring at me.

"Water, please," I say, realizing just how dry my mouth has become.

A concerned look crosses his face, and I realize that my skin is flush again. "You okay, Mia? You need to sit down or something?" Concern etches in the furrow of his eyebrows.

I take a moment to gather my thoughts before saying, "I'm fine, just parched." I look into those golden hazel eyes, and the last of the moisture in my body soaks my panties.

The sun makes the gold glow in his eyes, and I look away to gather myself. *What the hell am I doing?* He walks over to steady me as I feel myself begin to sway a little. Inhaling his scent in this close proximity makes me clinch my thighs together. His hand swipes down my back before stopping right above the tattoo on my lower back, and I can feel my heartbeat in my panties.

"Contracts?" I say as I pull away from him and clear my throat.

He smiles down at me, holding the bottle of water out to me. Grabbing the bottle of water from his hand, our pinkies touch, and I think back to all the movies that I have seen where the lovers lift their pinkies, reaching out to the person their heart truly desires. This isn't that though. This is Sincere. My friend. We aren't that.

When I hear him clear his throat, it jolts me from my thoughts. Smiling nervously, I realize I missed whatever he just asked, again. "I'm sorry, my mind was somewhere else. What did you say?"

He runs his hands down his waves, and I grow seasick looking at him. Instead of repeating himself, he grabs the water bottle from my hands and opens it and hands it back. Closing my eyes, I take a long sip, allowing the coolness of the water to reduce the blazing temperature of my body. Opening my eyes, I realize that he's watching me drink the water.

Something unfamiliar to me flickers in his eyes, but as soon as it appears, it's gone with a blink. Under his gaze, my body burns. And I realize that I'm in trouble.

How the hell am I going to get through this deal without making G's dumb ass right?

CHAPTER FOUR

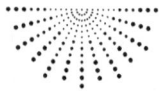

*A*fter signing the contract in Sincere's office, I sit back in my white chair and look at him across the white and gold marble table. His office is beautiful. I can tell that he had it professionally designed, and whoever he hired knew their stuff. I make it a mental note to ask for the designer's information.

"Did you have any additional questions about anything not outlined in the contracts?" As he speaks, his gaze ignites me all over again. It's like being in his presence makes the fight that I had just seem more valid. This makes me begin to resent the fact that I was accused of something that in my mind wasn't a possibility, but my body screams that it's damn near mandatory.

Wait until I tell Maya about this shit. I already know she's going to want me to jump this man's bones.

"I have nothing further about the contracts, but can we talk about Kimber and her crazy ass accusations?"

The mention of his wife instantly puts me on ice, and I can tell that my words did the same for him. Sincere sighs before he rises from his side of the table and crosses the room to his bar. It's stocked with his favorite bourbon and the finest top shelf liquors, cigars, and a pretty great wine collection. He opens the decanter and begins making himself an old fashioned.

"You know it's not even noon yet," I say, chuckling and spinning in my chair to face him.

As he completes the cocktail, he pulls out a martini glass and begins to make me a dry ginger martini with a hint of lime. *He remembers my drink?* When we were in Vegas, he offered to order us a drink at the bar, and I ordered this very drink. The bartender named it the Mama Mia because of the spice of the ginger. Crossing the room, he sips his drink and places mine in front of me, then he takes a seat on the large plush couch that sits offset from the conference table.

Inhaling the ginger, I sip the drink, and it's delicious. "Since we're going to be working together, let me lay some ground rules." His tone is serious but command-ing. "Going forward, when you're in my office, you don't speak of Kimber. Yes, she is my wife, for now, but it seems like that doesn't matter to either of us, being that your pussy is leaking for me right now."

I choke on the martini that I was savoring. "Wh—what the fuck are you talking about Sincere?" I manage to stammer out in between deep inhales.

"Mia, it's just you and I here, and nobody is going to bother us in my space. Not even Lesley. You don't have to pretend like you don't know what it is between us. We were always meant to be together, but our lives didn't align that way. I let you have your fun with Giavonni, even though I wanted to snap his neck every time I saw a new social media post of him with the side bitch of the month. All of that shit is coming to an end now. Especially since he is fucking my "wife" as you put it."

As his words sink in, I realize that every interaction that we've had over the years has been intentional. Down to us seeing each other while we were in Vegas.

Wait. Did he just say G is fucking Kimber?

"Hold the fuck on, Cere. What do you mean Giavonni is fucking Kimber? He didn't even—"

Before I can finish my sentence, a screen illuminates on the wall behind the bar with a video of two people fucking. It doesn't take me long to realize that it is definitely Giavonni's ass, and he is balls deep in Kimber. Jumping up from my seat and grabbing my phone at the same time I head over to the screen. Seething with betrayal, I look down at my phone to call this cheating, lying bastard, but then I stop and spin around and can see the glint of amusement in Sincere's eyes.

"How long have you known about this? Did you know yesterday when I called you?"

The nod of his head confirms he was indeed withholding this information yesterday.

"They have been seeing each other for about sixteen months now."

The timeline in my head crashes into me like déjà vu. That's when he started to go to rehab at that fucking clinic.

"Did he meet her at the clinic?" My tone is filled with a calm rage that I don't recognize but I embrace it all the same.

"Kimber. Is. The. Physical. Therapist," he says in a calm voice.

"Why now? Why didn't you say something before now?" The confusion mixed with anger causes me to stammer a bit on my words.

"I wanted to make sure that when I told you about it that he couldn't deny it. If I had told you this over the phone, would you have believed me?"

Pausing, I think about what he's asking me and how I would have reacted if he did indeed try to tell me. "I can't say for certain that I would have believed you if you told me without this video, but what I can say for certain is that I don't appreciate how you ambushed me with this."

Clenching my fist, I'm reminded that my phone is in my hand.

Sincere stands and walks over to me. Grabbing me around the waist, he pulls me closer to him. "Listen, Mia. I wanted to make sure that we're on the same page because I have a plan, and I need your help with it."

My heart feels like it will beat out of my chest as I take in his words and try to process my emotions. "Plan. You had time to make a fucking plan, but you didn't have time to tell me what the fuck was going on with our spouses?"

I'm still seething at this point, and Sincere's grasp loosens at my words.

"I didn't want to bring you no half-assed story. I needed to make sure that what I thought was a fact. Do you know how bad you would have cursed me out if I didn't have proof?" His cool and even tone provides a sense of protection, and it's been a while sense I've felt that.

"What makes you think I'll be willing to go along with your plan?" While he has my interest, I don't want him to think that I will give in so easily.

"Because I've seen the messages where he plans to take half of everything when you find out and try to leave him."

At this point, I've heard enough, and I need to get out of this office before I lose my fucking mind. "Look, I need to go. I thank you for the information, but I don't want to be involved in any plan that you've made. I will take my chances with G in court because everything that I have is protected."

Turning to leave, I can feel my anger starting to resurface, but Sincere's parting words push it up and out.

"Well, you should know that my wife told me this morning that she's pregnant. The only problem is I can't have kids, so there is only one other person that could be the father."

Moving faster, I push his words to the back of my mind until I'm back in my car.

CHAPTER FIVE

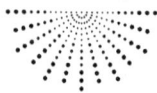

"*H*ow did the meeting go?" Maya asks as she picks up the phone.

"Fuck the meeting. Giavonni has been fucking Kimber." I can feel myself saying the words out as I pull out onto the highway, but it is still surreal.

"What the fuck do you mean?!" she screams.

My mind races as I try to gather my thoughts to explain things to Maya. "Are you at the office or are you at home?"

I wait for her response as I sit in the intersection. "I just got home. I'm taking a mental health day."

Maya's words are the compass that I follow straight to her house. Pulling into her driveway, I know there's no going home tonight, and it will be a long rest of the day, processing all the information I just received. As I climb out of my car, I look at my phone. There's a message from Sincere with a video attachment. I can already tell that it is the same video, based on the paused view.

I immediately forward the video to Maya and power down my phone. When I walk into the house, I can hear the video playing with the sounds of Maya screaming about how much of a "dawg ass nigga" Giavonni is.

"What kind of shit is this?"

When she finally looks up from the phone, I'm already in the kitchen looking for the biggest wine glass I can find. When I don't see one that's large enough, I just walk over and open my favorite wine and start to drink if from the bottle.

"So, you want to talk about it, or do you need a minute?" Maya asks as she comes closer to me and hands me a wine glass. Instead of taking the glass, I walk to the living room, ready to tell her about all the bullshit that has unfolded.

When I finish, she sits there, dumbfounded for a second before she lights into his ass.

"So wayment. You mean to tell me that this nigga knew they were fucking around and didn't say shit to you yesterday when you called him about her allegedly writing G?"

Reaching over for the bottle of wine again, I nod my

head in agreement. After telling her the entire story uninterrupted, there was nothing left to say.

"So did he tell you what the fucking plan is that he has in mind?"

Looking out the window I shake my head no before saying, "I really didn't want to know any of this shit. And the fact that he already had a damn plan pissed me off. Imagine being in the presence of a man that God definitely took his time on, smelling like he just stepped out of heaven. Feeling your panties become soaked then seeing something that takes you from Aquafina to the Sahara Desert. Had me standing there with wet panties feeling like I had just pissed myself in public."

As I continue, I can see the disgust on Maya's face out the corner of my eye. "I don't know what he expected from me. It was like one minute I was chilling with a friend, and the next I was devastated and in fucking shock. I would never want to see my man fucking another woman. Like why the fuck did he think I would want to see that?"

Maya exhales when I finish speaking, and I look at her because I know she has something to say. "Well, you know that there was a time that nobody could tell you shit about G and you actually believe it."

Rolling my eyes I let her continue.

"That man has drug you through the dirt. You take

care of everything. You are cooking, cleaning, washing clothes, maintaining vehicles, paying the bills, booking flights, fucking, sucking, and that's all for him before you even start to do anything for yourself. Girl, you remember when he got his first big check from the league and your car was stolen and he let you catch the bus for six months, but he bought him and his big back ass mammy brand new cars? Paid cash at that. Or how about when that bald headed Tatiana wrote you telling you every way he had her bent up but you ain't want to listen until your ass was burnt. Got me holding your hand while they put that big ass needle in your ass, knowing I'm squeamish."

As she recounts all the fucked-up things that I have just let slide over the years, I realize that I've been the fucking fool. And here I was again being made out to look like a damn dummy by the man that was supposed to be my forever.

"You're right. I have let way too much slide, and I thought that I would be more hurt by all of this, but if I am honest, I am not even mad. I am just tired. I can't do this shit anymore. And to think he really out here fucking that man wife and has the fucking balls to accuse me of sleeping with Sincere," I say before tossing back the last of the wine.

"So, what do you want to do, boo? Because I will set some shit up if you got your life insurance in order." We both burst out laughing because Maya was always watching way too much ID channel.

"First of all, you know life insurance is on auto draft for that damn daredevil. And second, calm down, heffa. We both know the best revenge is to just let them go and miss you."

Maya jumps up off the couch at my words. "Naw, bitch, cut the WE shit. 'We' is inclusive, and I ain't included in that shit. So, we don't know anything about any of that. You always want to give some ole healed-ass answer to his fuck nigga moves. What I do know is you hit a man in the pockets if you want to get even. Or fuck his daddy and make a son that his daddy could be proud of."

I burst out laughing because I can always depend on Maya to give me the real and make me laugh. "Therapy is doing me well, and if I'm honest with myself for once, I can say that I already knew that this day was coming. Waiting on the other shoe to drop got to be tiring, so I stopped and started operating as if it already had. That has really helped me start to heal."

Glancing over at the clock, I notice that it's now eight o'clock at night, and we've been talking about this since this morning. "Girl, is it really eight? We need to get some food. No wonder I can't feel my face. I haven't eaten anything all day," I say reaching for my purse to hit up Uber Eats. The doorbell causes me to pause and look over at Maya who stands up and heads for the door.

"Girl, I ordered food twenty minutes ago. You know I was not about to have you in here, three sheets to the wind, and not feed you." She grabs the food and comes back into the room holding bags from two of my favorite places to indulge in when I am eating my emotions. China One's House Lo Mein with braised lemon Pepper wings and Fiesta Lime Chicken with Shrimp Parmesan on top with loaded mashed potatoes and a gallon of strawberry Long Island Iced Tea from Applebee's. My girl knows me all too well. I was about to spend too much damn time trying to figure out which one I wanted to eat, and here she is making life easier on me.

"Why choose when you can have it all?" Maya says, sitting the bags down.

Reaching over, I hug her tight, "You are the best friend that a girl could pray for." My vision grows blurry as I hold back tears.

"Go ahead and get the release cry in so you don't cry in your mashed potatoes." As the tears begin to cascade down my face, I can only laugh at the incident that she's referring to. When we were in college, I got drunk for the first time and ended up crying at our table at Applebee's because my potatoes had sour cream, and I was allergic. I just cried at the table until the waitress came and took the plate away when Maya explained to them what was going on. I'm sure they thought that I was crazy after that, but they never got my order wrong again.

"Look, this impromptu girl's day was needed, and we will enjoy the rest of tonight, but tomorrow you have to turn that phone back on and face the music. If you want to leave, I'll book the movers. If you want to stay, I will keep your Visine supply stocked. If you just need time, I'll be your timekeeper. I'm here for you girl, just let me know what we're doing, and we can go from there. You are not alone in this. Now hand me that damn remote so we can catch up on Reasonable Doubt so we can find out if Jax is going to leave Lewis' trifling ass. And she better, because fuck him, that baby, and its too hot to trot ass mammy."

Getting comfortable on the couch again, I open the Lo Mein and dive right in.

CHAPTER SIX

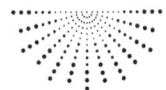

The sound of Maya getting her back broke in wakes me up out of my sleep. At first, I think that I'm dreaming, but as her loud ass screams get louder, I realize that Chris' ass must have come to blow her back out. I sit up on the couch and look for my purse to finally turn my phone on when I feel the gush, reminding me yet again this month that I'm not pregnant.

Jumping up from the couch I go into my room and get some clothes to wear. It's moments like these that I appreciate Maya for having a bedroom in her home just for me. It has clothes that are my size and style as well as everything that I would need as if I lived here. Walking into the ensuite bathroom, I turn on the shower as hot as I can get it to prepare to scrub the last ten years off. Looking in the closet, I grab one of my dark towel sets and my honey pot wash along with a Pink Rose Dove bar and head back to the shower. Stepping out of my pajamas that I put on before we started watching Practical Magic, I notice that I have completely soaked my pants. I look at the floor and there are bloody footprints in the bathroom from the closet to the tub. I climb in the shower and press the button on the side panel next to it. A blinding pain shoots through my back and butt, and I don't know what to do. I scream because it feels like I am being ripped in half. It seems like forever goes by before Maya shows up at the bathroom door.

The smile on her face is immediately replaced with fear. "Please help me, My. I'm hurting so bad."

Maya looks around the room, and I can only scream from the pain that I am in. Chris comes running into the bathroom, and she springs into action.

"Where is the pain, Mia?" she says climbing into the shower with me.

"Everywhere!" I yell at her.

"Show me." Her voice is calm, and it makes me want to calm down to answer her.

Running my hand across my back and abdomen she asks me the dumbest question I've ever heard. "When was your last period?"

By this time, I'm in pain and utterly frustrated with

the stupidity that I'm surrounded with. "Clearly I am having a period right now," I say back in between cramps.

"This is not a period. We need to get you to the hospital. I think you might be experiencing a tubal pregnancy. We need to stop this bleeding."

Maya comes back with her phone and EMS in tow. The pain is so bad that I didn't even hear her leave or call anyone. Maya hands me a robe, and Chris lets them know that they will be right behind me.

The journey to the hospital is one of the scariest trips I've ever experienced. Every bump hurts, every touch hurts, and still I'm numb due to the fact that I may be having an ectopic pregnancy. As they push me inside, the nurses rush me to the maternity floor. Never in a million years did I think this would be the reason that I headed to this floor.

They perform an ultrasound where they conclude that the pregnancy isn't ectopic, but I'm in natural labor. When they turn off the monitor instead of showing me my baby, I panic. Why would they do that? Chris and Maya burst into the room as they set the room up for me to begin pushing. Everything happens so fast that I don't want to do anything but process.

Chris is now gowned up, being that she's the real-life Addison Montgomery from Grey's Anatomy. She moves the current LPN aside as she soothes me and walks me through what to do next.

"Mia, I need you to push for me. I know that this is going to hurt, but I need you to just push for me." Maya walks over to my side, holding my hand as Chris continues to give directions. "Good job, I need you to push just like that for me one more time."

I feel like somebody has lit a match to my ass, and I hurt so bad. I feel the biggest relief as the baby comes out. As relief washes over me, it's quickly overshadowed by the silence in the room. I watch as Chris hands the baby off to a nurse.

When I feel my body start to grow in pain again. Chris presses on my stomach, and I can feel something else as it slides out of me. When I see what appears to be a second baby still in the sac, I freak out. I know that thing did not come out of me. It couldn't have. These are the things that I see when I am watching TLC shows about baby deliveries.

"Why are they so small? Why aren't they crying?" My voice comes out as a whisper even though I scream the questions over and over in my head.

"Let them work, babe. You're okay," Maya says holding my hand.

Everything happened so fast that they had no real time to hook me to any of the machines all around me. "My, something is wrong. I don't feel right."

The room begins to spin, and I can no longer hang on to consciousness.

A BEEPING SOUND wakes me up. As I open my eyes, I quickly remember the events that took place. I look around the room and see G sitting in a chair that's too small for his large frame, playing his PlayStation. Maya is next to my bed on a pull-out cot, staring at her phone.

Attempting to sit up, a pain in my abdomen makes me fall back. Maya rushes over to me. "Relax, babe. Everything's okay. You're okay." She presses a button above my head for the nurse.

"How can I help you?" The nurse's voice was soft and gentle.

"She's awake. Can you send in Dr. Frazier?" Maya looks down at me and winks. Maya walks over to the TV and turns it off, and G gets ready to fly off the handle, but when Maya points to me, he quickly spins around realizing he has missed something. Before he can come over to me, Dr. Christina Frazier walks in with a chaplain and nurse. My heart sinks, because I know whatever is about to follow is going to devastate me.

"Is it okay to speak in front of everyone present?"

Chris asks, looking me in my eyes and glancing over at G. As I nod my head yes, she begins. "Can I just have you verify your name and date of birth for me please before we start?"

Chris grabs my hand and looks down at my armband.

"Her name is A'Mia Lynn Wallace. Born on July 14th, 1994," Giavonni chimes in.

I clear my throat before Chris can interject. "My full name is A'Mia Lynn Jones. Birthday is June 14th, 1994."

Chris thanks me for the clarification with a head nod before she begins. "Yesterday was a pretty hectic day for you. I want to walk you through everything that happened. Please feel free to stop me at any time if you don't understand something, or if you just need a moment."

Nodding my head in confirmation, I wait for Chris to begin.

"So, you mean to tell me all this time you haven't had my fucking last name?"

Everyone turns to look at Giavonni. "Your ass can not be fucking serious right now. She's laying in the fucking hospital and could have fucking died yesterday, and that is all that you care about is your weak ass last name. G, I swear to all that is unholy I will have them call security for your goof troop looking ass, if you don't let this doctor speak to your wife in fucking peace."

Maya's reply stuns us all, but part of me knows she's serious. G's face turns sour, but he doesn't open his mouth.

"A'Mia, what you went through is called Placenta previa. It is when the placenta grows over part or all of the cervix opening. This can cause an extremely higher risk of postpartum hemorrhage. Because you didn't know that you were pregnant, you didn't know that you were slowly tearing your placenta away from the uterine wall. In your case, your placenta was not covering the full opening of the cervix, but the influx of blood let us know we would have to deliver the babies as quickly as possible and then try to stop the bleeding. There are many reasons that this can happen."

I hold up my hand to stop her. "Could this have happened because of scar tissue in the uterus?" I look over at G to see if he is processing any of this.

"Yes, that is very possible." Tears begin to roll down my face as I let her continue. "You were about twenty-eight weeks pregnant with fraternal twins. One boy, one girl. Your son came out first. Your daughter followed, but she was born in what we call a veiled birth. That is when the amniotic sac does not rupture and is delivered intact. We believe your son's sac broke which led to starting your labor. With the labor starting, it also caused the placenta to begin to rupture as well, causing the cord to be wrapped around his neck, and he was born sleeping."

My heart shatters at her words. The sound that escapes me is one that I didn't know was humanly possible. Maya climbs into the bed with me and pulls me into her arms.

How did I not know I was pregnant?

"Let's give her a minute," Maya tells Chris.

"No," I yell louder then intended. "Break my heart once. I'm not sure I will be able to take anything else if you stop now." My words plead for Chris to continue.

"We broke your daughter's sac to get her out and take her to the NICU. But you started to bleed, so you became my priority. We had to rush you into surgery because you did begin to hemorrhage after you delivered the placenta. Because of how much damage was done, we had to do a partial hysterectomy. We didn't remove your ovaries."

I already knew that she was going to say this, but I only have one concern. "What about my daughter? Please tell me she made it."

I feel Maya's body tense as if she's bracing for me to fall apart all over again. "Baby girl Jones is in the NICU, and she is fighting for her life. Her lungs are underdeveloped, so we will be keeping her for quite a while. We will take you down to see her when you are ready."

I can tell by the way Maya relaxes that she's hearing the news for the first time as well.

"We have an extra wrist band for access to the unit. Would you like us to put it on you now, Daddy?" the nurse asks, walking over to G.

He looks over at me and then at the nurse. "I might not even be the daddy. My last name is fucking Wallace, not Jones." He brushes past the nurse, knocking shit over as he leaves.

That is the last fucking straw for me. It will be a chilly day in hell before I ever exist in a marital space with that fucking human again!

CHAPTER SEVEN

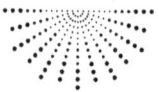

"*Mina* Joy, it's your mommy. I love you so much, pretty girl," I say as I look at my tiny daughter. She's only two-and-a-half pounds and can fit in the palm of my hand. I'm still in awe that I was able to carry not one but two babies after years of fertility issues due to having a botched abortion in college.

Giavonni told me he didn't want to have kids after signing with the Falcons his junior year of college ball. It wasn't until four years in the league and after our first year of marriage that I realized something was wrong. We tried for over a year with no luck. At my annual, I found out that one of my fallopian tubes needed removing because it was fused closed. It was during this time that I had an oblation of my uterus because of scar tissue from all those years ago. After my surgery, my doctor let me know that I may not be able to have children, but because I came from a praying family, I knew God would have the last say so.

"There goes auntie baby," Maya says walking in, loud and proud as usual. This girl has been my rock, and I am so grateful for all the support she has given me.

"Look MiMi, Auntie My is here." My baby girl doesn't respond, but I know that we just have to keep talking to her. We sit and listen to Gracie's Corner at Maya's request until I finish pumping. They're still spoon-feeding her, but still encourage me to pump so that she gets breast milk with her feedings. As we go back to my room, the elevator is quiet with the unspoken decisions that were very necessary at this point.

When we get back to my room, Maya opens the door, and I am in shock to find my room covered in flowers. "What is all of this?" I say as tears cloud my vision.

"Don't start them damn tears. These are all from Sincere. He's been sending them to the office, but I figured that you could use some good energy in this room as well."

I look at all the different purple roses in different phases of life. Some are in full bloom, while others are just starting to bud. I can't help but appreciate the thought behind the roses.

"I brought your cell and a charger. I see you never checked your messages from Tuesday."

Looking over at the calendar, I realize that it is Friday, and I have not checked my phone, nor have I had the desire to. Reaching for my phone, I look at the home screen and immediately grow sick to my stomach. Seeing Giavonni's face pressed into my neck makes me want to throw this phone across the room.

"Send me that picture you took of Mina," I say to Maya. My phone dings, and I immediately change my lock screen to my baby girl.

"Babe, I have to ask you some questions. I know that you may not be in the mindset, but this can't wait."

Looking over at her, I'm confused about what the fuck could be so pressing.

"We need to make the arrangements for your son."

My heart skips a beat, and I realize that I can't even deal with that.

"I have already done most of it. I just need to make sure that everything is the way you would want it." She sits on the bed and shows me all the plans that she has made for my baby boy. Her phone rings, and I see that it is the funeral home calling. She answers on speaker so that we can both hear.

"Hello. Am I speaking with Maya Green?" the gentleman on the phone asks.

"Yes, this is she. I'm also sitting with the mother, A'Mia Jones," she answers him so that he can address us both.

"Okay, great. Ms. A'Mia, we are so sorry for your loss. Your husband has handled all of the costs. He also gave us the go ahead to cremate baby Giavonni so we have started that process. I just want wanted to—"

Cutting the old man off, I scream, "He did *what*?!"

Maya jumps out of the bed to begin to fix this. "Wait, sir. There has to be some kind of mix-up. She hasn't even seen the baby."

My stomach drops as I think about when they asked me if I wanted to see my son. "I told them no because I thought I had more time. I wasn't ready to have to say goodbye, and I thought I would be able to when I was ready. Giavonni has taken that away from me as well. He named my son after him after saying that he wasn't sure it was his fucking baby. What kind of sick mind game is he fucking playing with me?"

My words are all jumbled as I ramble while looking over at all the flowers in the room. I climb slowly out of the bed and throw one of the vases at the wall. When the first one shatters, Maya jumps out of the way when she realizes that I have already tossed the second one.

She walks over to me and hugs me, holding my hands to my sides so that I can't throw anything else.

"Is everything alrig—" the nurse walks in asking but stops when she looks and sees the room. She looks at me with sad eyes. "Do you need anything?"

"I need the birth certificate paperwork for my daughter, and I want it processed as soon as possible. And if any man comes up here to see me or my baby, you are to call security and have him escorted off the premises!" My voice is calm despite the rage that churns in my belly. I could fucking kill G for this shit. All he has ever done is hurt me. One fucking thing after another. But this, this is a new low, even for him!

The old me could forgive and love through the pain, but the bitch that I am today could never love this kind of man, not even if he thought he could change. "Niggas and flies I do despise, the more I know niggas, the more I like flies."

CHAPTER EIGHT

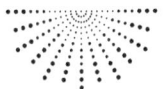

*M*aya and I walk into the house that I shared with Giavonni for the past ten years of my life. The large clock on the wall read 07:42 a.m., ensuring that I have time to get what I need before the movers arrive. Everything was the same as it was when I left for work three weeks ago, letting me know that Giavonni hadn't been here to let the housekeepers in the house. I walk into my bedroom and my bed is made on my side, but the sheets are crumpled where G got out the bed without making it as usual.

Walking into my closet, I pull out my luggage before opening the safe that I had installed while G was on the road one year. I look in the folder that I keep in the safe and take out all my personal effects.

"The movers are here," Maya says from the front of

the house where she's probably raiding the wine cabinet.

"Great. The gate code is two, two, six, seven," I shout back so that she can let them in and I can get this done as quickly as possible. After finding out the foul shit that Giavonni had done to my son, I made it my business to use all my resources to keep my daughter away from him.

We had Mina transferred to the children's hospital which was more suited to help with her development and was also close to Maya's home and the home that I had owned for the past two years. As the movers come in and pack all of my personal belongings and load them in the moving truck, I'm so relieved that G hasn't come home during the process.

Cee-Lo Green's "Fuck You" starts playing from my phone, alerting me to the monster-in-law that was ringing my line.

"Hello?" I answer flatly.

"Hey, Ms. Priss. How are you doing?" Her voice has always annoyed the shit out me. She's one of those mothers who don't believe her precious baby boy could ever do anything wrong.

"I'm good, but busy. Did you need something?" Maybe rushing her to tell me what she wants will help me to avoid the bullshit that is sure to ensue if we stay on the phone too long.

"Oh, I didn't want anything. I saw G the other day, and he looked thinner than usual. I just wanted to make sure everything was good in the home." Her accusing tone is all that I need to unload everything on her ass here and now.

"Well let's see. Where should I start?"

She cuts in before I can say anything else. "See I knew your ass had done something to my baby. What the hell did you do this time?"

Fighting back the urge to curse her out, I decide to hit her where it hurts. She has always wanted grandchildren and has always made it a big deal that I hadn't given her any. Now is my time to shine and fuck her world up in the process.

"Actually, I went into premature labor with twins after finding out that your son has yet again been cheating on me, and my sweet baby boy died. My daughter is in the NICU, and your trifling, good-for-nothing son decided to cremate my son before I ever got a chance to hold him in my arms."

The phone goes silent.

"What's wrong? You have no smart-ass comeback for your son being the scum of the fucking earth?" I wait for a few more seconds before I continue. "Your son made you a grandmother, but as far as my daughter, you will never get to meet her. Maybe his side bitch that is also currently pregnant can give you that title because my child will never call you that!"

I hang up and let the old bitch stew on that shit. I take one last look around the house before walking out and leaving my key on the island. Walking over to the garage, I grab three sets of keys off the rack. I toss one to Maya, and the other two to Chris and her brother A'Meir.

"Yall follow me."

As they press the unlock buttons on the vehicles, they all make faces of excitement. Maya instructs the movers to follow me, and we all pull out of the driveway of the space I shared for far too long with the man that taught me that forever does have an end date.

Pulling to the gate of my new community, I drive into the guard area to let them know just how many vehicles will be with me and let them know my address. I swipe my access badge and lead the four vehicles following me to my new home. Pulling into the driveway of my home, I wait for everyone to pull in behind me. While unlocking the house, the smell of warm cinnamon and vanilla greets me. It instantly pulls a relaxing breath from me. I didn't even realize there were still unbroken parts of me until I walked into a house that I owned outright and paid for with my money and in my name.

A'Meir is the first to enter, handing me the keys to

the pearl white BMW 760i. "That is a nice car..." He pauses because we haven't been formally introduced.

"You can call me Mia. Nice to officially meet you." Smiling at him, I grab the keys and place them on the counter.

"Pleasure is all mine. Where do you need me?" he asks as he walks back towards the door.

"Um. I guess you can start by me showing you where most of this stuff is going to go." Leading him to the stairs, he follows me up, and I show him where my closet is.

He whistles. "You got some taste, girl." His tone is amusing as we walk deeper into the closet.

"Bags and hats will go here," I say pointing to the space to my left.

"Heels will go here." I point to the custom-built gallery setting I have for all my heels that I don't wear.

"Business/Fashion pieces will go over there," I say pointing to the sectioned closet for clothes.

"And over here is where I will spend most of my time grabbing items." We walk into the other closet that I had made just for athletics. There are three walls with built-in shoe cubbies for all my current exclusive sneakers. On the other side is an area for all my sweat suits, jeans, and athletic leggings and sports tanks.

"Well dang, girl. No, his and hers in here, huh?"

I chuckle as I hear My and Chris looking for us. "I

know I better have my own room in this big ass house," Maya says as we walk out of the closet and meet them in the bathroom.

"You have your own suite, Maya. It's not even part of the main house."

Her eyes grow so big at the revelation that she gets the guest house. "Bitch, I know I said that I better have a guest house when you make it big, but I didn't think you would actually go through with it," she says, heading back the way she came.

While she may not have believed I would give her the guest house, she isn't about to not go see what it has to offer. "Wait. Before you go down there, can you help me direct traffic with the movers? I need to call and check on Mina."

"Girl, yes. Just to be clear, you want this set up just like we talked about, right?" Maya asks while she heads for the stairs.

"Yes, just tell them not to go into any of the rooms on the other side. I want to set her room up myself."

Shaking her head while giving me a reassuring smile, she heads downstairs with Chris and A'Meir in tow.

After checking in on my baby girl, it was time to pump so that I can make sure that when my baby does come home she has a healthy supply of milk. Glancing at the counter, I notice that Chris and Maya placed their keys down next to where I had laid the others. I grab all three and head around the house to get to the garage.

"Don't you drop that or you going to have an issue walking when you leave," I hear Maya tell one of the movers.

"Play nice, Maya. They're paid to be here and move things, not be yelled at by a mean midget."

The man looks at me, tilting his head in appreciation at my words.

"You say that now, but who are you going to complain to if anything is broken? Oh, yea, me."

I roll my eyes as I continue around the house. Rounding the corner to the garage, I notice that all the cars are already backed into the garage in the exact order that I would have put them in. I walk over to my matte black G-Wagon and see that A'Meir is pairing the garage door opener built into the car.

"So, I guess you found a way to make yourself useful?" I ask, climbing into the passenger side.

He looks up and smiles and those white teeth and dimples do something to me. "I figured it would be better to do this than to be yelled at by Maya. I don't know how Chris does it."

We both chuckle at the sound of Maya still barking orders. "Wait, how are you programming this if I have the keys?" I ask, realizing that I'm still holding all my keys.

"Did you take a good look at your keys or just pick them up?"

I look down at the key fobs in my hand and notice that there is only one fob on each ring. Looking back up at him, I smile and begin to say, "In an emergency, knowing where your keys are—"

He finishes my sentence, "—can be the difference between life and death."

My curiosity is piqued by him knowing this. "My mom used to tell me that when I was little," I share with him.

"Maya has said it so much to Chris that now Chris is saying it. One day it really was the difference for us. When our nephew was having a seizure, I jumped in the driver seat while Chris and his mother were in the back. Because the keys were already in the car, it made a difference in that moment."

I smile but jolt out of the moment by My and her annoying antics. "A'Meir and A'Mia sitting in the tree, f-u-c—"

I have to stop her before she finishes. "Alright, that's enough, heffa. Let's go and leave the man to his programming," I say, jumping out of the car to stop her from doing anything else to embarrass me.

"Do I need to arrange a double date with us? I saw that big ass smile you had plastered on your face."

Rolling my eyes at her, I walk back towards the house. "Girl, I'm not trying to date anyone. I'm just now wrapping my head around becoming a mother." I stop in my tracks when I realize what I just said. *I really am a mother.* My eyes swell with tears, and I brush them away as they begin to fall.

"Let's go see your house," I say brushing the last of the tears away and smiling at my friend. We interlock arms, and I take her to the guest house so she can see just how much of an auntie she is about to become.

CHAPTER NINE

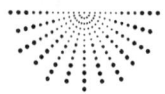

"Thank you so much for all of your help today," I say as I lay on the couch in my new home.

Chris, Maya, and A'Meir all reply with mouths full of pizza. "Why would you wait until we had a mouth full of food to say that?" Maya asks, wiping the sauce from her mouth.

"You act like I can see y'all from here."

Maya made me lay down seven times today while saying. "Either you can sit down or get set back!" Frustrated, I complied because Chris would always nod her head, letting me know that I needed to just let her win.

A'Meir comes around the back of the couch and hands me a plate with grilled chicken, asparagus, and a small kale salad with honey vinaigrette. I look at him like he has two heads. "Where is my pizza?" I ask frowning at the plate.

"You're nursing, and you need plenty of protein and healthy leafy veggies to help with lactation." My heart speeds up, and I realize that he's right. Reluctantly, I sit up and grab the plate.

He takes a seat beside me and places a glass of White-Cran-Strawberry juice on a coaster on my table. When I attempt to spin around so I can place my plate on the table, he stops me. "Didn't I hear Maya say you just had surgery?" he asks, grabbing my legs.

"Yes, but... What are you doing?"

He places a pillow on his lap before resting my feet across his legs. "You need to keep your feet elevated when you aren't on them."

Unsure of how to respond, I just shake my head and begin to eat. Biting into the chicken, it is the best thing that I have ever tasted. My eyes roll back, and I can feel him staring at me. When I come down from my foodgasm, we lock eyes.

"Is it that good?" He finds amusement in how much I enjoy this food.

"It is. Where did you order it? I'm going to have to order again and kiss the chef too."

He smiles and says, "Well only one of those things would be possible."

Looking at him in confusion I ask, "Why is that?"

Chris interrupts from the kitchen, providing the answer that I'm not expecting. "Because he made it just for you. Now kiss the chef!" Maya bursts out laughing, and I damn near choke on the piece of asparagus I just put in my mouth. How was I so distracted that I didn't even see this man in my kitchen cooking, let alone smell it. It had to be while Maya directed traffic in my closet.

A'Meir hands me the glass on the table to help wash down the food trapped in my throat.

"For somebody with no gag reflex, you sure do choke a lot."

A glint of something gleams in A'Meir's eyes at Maya's words. I know she didn't just say that shit.

"Alright everybody out." I take back possession of my feet from A'Meir and place the glass and plate on the table. "Maya has officially gotten y'all kicked out my house."

A'Meir stands from the couch, and I can feel the heat of his body as he rises to his full height. Looking over at him, I take in his breath-taking beauty. His smooth mocha skin has a honey glow, and his dimples compliment his chiseled jaw line. His locs are neatly kept and frame his face perfectly. I can see every muscle sculpted under his still white t-shirt. His body is etched in African art, and I pray he can't see my nipples in this thin ass tank top. He bends down and grabs my glass and plate before brushing past me to get to the kitchen. This man. Mmmm mmm mmm.

A'Meir looks at me and I know he can see that I want him. "Alright guys, let's get this mess cleaned up so she doesn't come in here and bust her stitches trying to do it."

I look from my living room to my kitchen and notice that the dishes are already in the dishrack drying, and there's just the mess from the pizza left.

"You busted your stitches, can't get your money from your bitches," Maya sings, and I burst out laughing.

"Maya and Chris, go ahead. I will finish up here and make sure everything is put up and secure."

"Maya, you can take one of my—" I start.

"No need. Chris has her car, and I have mine." A'Meir says as he continues to clean the kitchen area.

I think back, trying to figure out when they had time to do any of this, but between pumping and watching my baby on her NICU View, I haven't been paying as close attention as I usually do. Clearing my throat, I interject.

"Um, no offense, A'Meir, but I don't know you like that to just be left in a house alone with you."

Smiling while he continues to clean, he says, "No offense taken. That's a good way to be. I'm a stranger in your home, so I'll finish this up and then we can all leave together."

Hearing him call himself a stranger just didn't sit right with me.

"Next time though, you might not want to eat a plate of food from somebody that you don't know like that. What if I didn't wash my chicken?"

We all burst out laughing at him as he finishes wiping down my cabinets and grabbing the trash.

"Your leftovers are in the fridge. The glass containers can be placed in the microwave when you're ready to heat it up. I also made you some steak bites and sweet potatoes and broccoli."

Who the hell is this man, and what part of Marvel's Multiverse did he fall from? "Tha, thank you. I really appreciate that," I say breathlessly.

A'Meir and Chris head out, and I look over at Maya. "Bitch, don't look at me like that. I'm about to walk Chris out, but I'm staying here because we are going to talk about this before you freak out."

Rolling my eyes, I turn to head into the kitchen. The Roomba on the floor scares the shit out of me. *Where the hell did that thing come from? I know I didn't have one of those.* Grabbing a bottle of water from the fridge, I realize that I never ordered groceries. As I open both sides of my fridge and my freezer, I see my fridge is fully stocked with healthy foods with a minimal amount of my favorite junk foods. I close the fridge and go to my walk-in pantry and realize that it, too, is stocked with everything that I could think of that I would need.

When I come out of the pantry, I'm curious as to what else is here that I didn't buy. The pots and pans are stainless steel and not the cheap shit that you get out of Wal-Mart. *What the hell is going on here?*

"Why the hell are you under the cabinet?" Maya asks, scaring the dog shit out of me.

"Maya, why would you scare me like that? What if I busted a stitch?"

She waves me off as she goes to a wine cooler that I didn't even notice before and grabs a bottle of wine. Rubbing my temples, I decide to go upstairs and shower before I lose my mind trying to figure out who did all of this.

After my shower, I find Maya in my bed already in her pajamas. "Alright, heffa. Start explaining. I know I didn't have these soft ass towels at my house, so I know you are up to something."

Maya's face lights up as she begins to wiggle in my bed. "So, as you know, I mentioned to Chris that you would basically be starting over."

With raised eyebrows, I nod in her direction for her to continue.

"Well, A'Meir happened to be over there when I told

her that you were going to need help with moving all your stuff and that you only wanted to take certain things from the house. He was happy to hear that you were doing better and that you were leaving that piece of fat shit ass husband of yours."

I burst out laughing while she continues. "Well, he told me that after you had ordered everything that you needed to let him see the list. And well, everything that you see in here that wasn't on your list, he bought."

Putting my hands on my hips I prepare to curse her slam out. One thing I have never needed is a man to take care of me, and she knows that. Giavonni threw way too many of his gifts in my face over the years, and I'd be damned if I was ever going to give another nigga the chance to do that to me.

"My, you know how I feel about that shit." My agitation is apparent when I sit down on the bed.

"He is not Giavonni, Mia. He only wants to help. He didn't even want you to know that he bought this stuff. He told me to tell you it was from me."

Her words shock me. I have never met a man who spent a dime that didn't want recognition for it. "What do you mean he didn't want you to tell me he bought it?"

She shrugs. "He said he knows what it's like to have to start over, and he just wanted to make the load lighter since you already have my little Mina Joy to worry about."

I pull out my phone and check my NICU View at the mention of my baby girl. She's resting under the UV light because she has gotten jaundice. Her breaths are less shallow today, and I feel like God is trying to show me that life is going to work out.

"Look. Get some rest. We are here for you to help you transition through all of this," Maya says turning the light off.

CHAPTER TEN

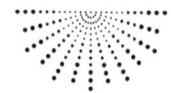

The tightness in my boobs wakes me, letting me know that it's time to pump. Climbing out of my bed, I go over to my pumping area that I set up near my balcony window. My shirt is soaked so I peel it over my head so I can get comfortable and relax while pumping. My phone pings on the nightstand, and I don't feel like getting up to get it. When it dings three more times, I know that these are active messages. When I get to the phone, I see that Giavonni's mother is blowing up my phone. Picking up the phone, I look at text preview on my lock screen.

> **Big Back Nappy Tracks:** Good Morning

> **Big Back Nappy Tracks:** Mia can you please talk to me?

> Big Back Nappy Tracks: When you get a chance, I want to sit down and talk.
>
> Big Back Nappy Tracks: The things you said yesterday were not what I was expecting to hear. I didn't raise Giavonni to be this hateful, and I won't stand for him doing such a thing to you.
>
> Big Back Nappy Tracks: Please call me when you are ready to talk. i love you.

I put the phone in my pocket. She can be added to the two hundred fifty-six messages from her son and Sincere that I'm not reading until I'm ready. My first pump is filled, so I put on my robe and head downstairs to my kitchen to empty the pumps into a storage bag.

I pull my phone out to connect to my sound system in the kitchen. The Bluetooth connects, and immediately Floetry starts to play. Turning to empty the pump into the bags, a sleepy Maya comes waltzing in the kitchen behind me.

"What are we going to eat? I want some pancakes." She looks a hot ghetto mess, talking about wanting some damn pancakes.

"Well, you can't get any looking like that."

She playfully nudges me. "Turn this hairy pussy music off. Hey, Siri, play TGIF by Glorilla."

The song blares through the speakers, and we start

to sing along. "I ain't got no nigga and no nigga ain't got..."

The song shuts off as Siri announces an incoming call. Maya walks over to the phone since my hands are still full trying to label the day on the milk. She swipes to answer the call, and I instantly get angry when I hear Giavonni's voice on Bluetooth.

"Nigga, why are you calling her?" Maya takes the phone and moves away from where I am, as I try to grab the phone to disconnect the call.

"Maya, hang up before he gets my location."

Her eyes grow wide, and she hangs up the call. "I'm sorry, boo. I wasn't thinking. I just wanted to curse him out for the old and the current. You know, say my piece."

Rolling my eyes, I grab my phone only for it to start ringing again. I look down and see that it is the number programmed for the guard station.

"Hello?" I answer, hoping that my punk ass baby daddy has not found his way here.

"Ms. Jones, we have a delivery for you."

Maya grins at me like she knows something I don't.

"Okay, let them in," I say, looking at Maya. She runs up the stairs, and I want to chase her black ass, but I see a black Mercedes Benz G63 leading two landscaping trucks up the long driveway. As they get closer to the house, I can see that A'Meir is in the backseat of the

Benz. Realizing that I'm still standing here, looking like the night before makes my feet spring into action. Heading up the stairs, I splash some water on my face, brush my teeth, and just as I finish dressing and pulling on the jacket to my red Nike track suit, my doorbell chimes.

Throwing some gloss on my lips, I pick up my phone to speak through my Ring camera. "How can I help you?" I ask as I pull my Jordan thirteens from the shelf and put them on my feet. I pass my perfume stand, doubling back to spray on some Gucci Guilty Gold to make sure that I smell as good as I look.

"I'll get it," Maya says, not knowing I already answered on my Ring camera. Just as he was about to say something, I heard my front door swing open. I have never been so thankful for knotless braids as I am now, because a messy top bun is all I'm able to do while heading down the stairs.

When I reach the foyer, I hear Maya and A'Meir talking, but his voice leaves the conversation when he sees me behind her.

"Well, shit." He moves around Maya and heads over to greet me.

"Good morning, A'Meir. What are you doing here? And why are those landscaping trucks with you?"

His smile makes my insides quiver as he stands there, looking like something straight out of GQ magazine. Peering at up at him, I know that he can feel my attraction to him, and it makes me feel bad. Why am I feeling like this about this man? He is a man for crying out loud. They all have one thing in mind. Wine, dine, then slide the panties to the side. I can't imagine anything else because I haven't experienced it before.

"I noticed some inconsistencies on the property line, and I would like to take care of that for you. I'll take you outside to meet my lead landscaper, Kareem." His voice is faint as the dream from last night plagues my mind.

Maya snaps her fingers in my face. "Earth to Mia. Did you hear any of that? Or..."

"Yes," I say, cutting her off. What the hell had I missed?

"Great, then let's go meet Kareem." Grabbing my hand, A'Meir leads me outside. His hand in mine feels good, like my hand was made to fit perfectly in his.

Snap out of it, Mia, you haven't even taken out the trash that is currently overflowing in your life.

The number of supplies that the men brought with them is like he already knew what I want. After instructing Kareem on my specific vision, I'm happy that he's able to immediately get to work.

Walking A'Meir out, I turn to him. "You can send me an invoice to the foundation email, and I will be sure that my office manager gets it paid."

He holds up his hand to stop me. "That won't be

necessary. This project is on the house. Like I said, I noticed a few faults in the lawn yesterday. I would sleep better knowing that I took this off your plate for you." The sincerity in his words makes me relax a little.

"Well, we wouldn't want this lawn to keep you up at night now, would we?" We both chuckle. "I have to get to the hospital, so I guess I will see you around. Thanks again for everything."

My words make that damn smile appear again and I get lost in those damn dimples.

"You need a ride over? I'm heading that direction if you don't feel like driving. I know yesterday was a lot on you." I want to say no, but I really don't feel like driving, and I know that Maya will be more than happy to pick me up when I'm ready to leave.

"Are you sure? I don't want to put you out of the way."

"Go get what you need so we can get you to your baby girl."

My feet begin to move, and Maya meets me at the door with my purse and my hospital bag that I always take when visiting Mina.

Why is it when this man says something, my body follows the command?

I'm going to kill this heffa because I know she has just been watching and listening on my damn Ring camera.

"Don't let your right now husband keep you from finding your forever."

Her words catch me off guard. Taken aback by them, I look at my friend and realize that now is my time to drop a major bomb on her since she is obviously helping A'Meir ambush me. "I never turned in my marriage license to the courthouse, so I don't have a right now husband and have never been married."

I can see the hamster start to race on the wheel when I rush off to climb in the car with A'Meir. "Let me grab that for you," he says as he grabs my bags and opens the door for me to climb in the backseat. He climbs in on the other side before reaching over to buckle my seatbelt. I take a moment to admire his vehicle and his taste. While we have similar G63, his has been customized for him to have extra space in the back seat. After settling in and telling him the name of the hospital, we pull out of my driveway to our next destination.

CHAPTER ELEVEN

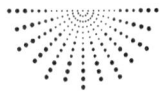

he journey to see my baby girl is a short one. Maya blows my text messages up, and I'm proud of myself for being able to successfully ignore her. A'Meir's driver gets out and opens the door for me as A'Meir climbs out, grabbing my bag.

"Thank you…" I trail off as I address the driver, waiting for him to tell me his name.

"Cliff, my name is Cliff," he replies, smiling then shaking my hand.

"Thank you, Cliff."

His smile gets brighter, and he shuts the door before walking around to A'Meir's side of the car. When I reach the other side, A'Meir stands there with my bag on his back like he's staying.

"I'll take that." Extending my hand, I wait for him to give me the bag, but he just smiles and grabs my hand.

"You're still not healed enough to be carrying bags on your back."

He leads me into the hospital, and I see Giavonni standing at the front desk. I'm not ready to deal with this shit, but I guess now is the best time. I attempt to let go of A'Meir's hand, but instead of heading to the desk, he leads me to the elevators. When the elevator dings, I step on with A'Meir at my back. Turning around, I lock eyes with Giavonni as the doors close. My heart sinks a little because I know it is about to be a shitshow, and I would rather it not be a scene. My face must show my thoughts because A'Meir speaks.

"Don't worry. He'll never make it to the floor with your daughter. He'll probably be escorted off the premises because they don't allow people who don't have the name of a patient to just loiter in the lobby."

I turn to look at him to better understand his words. It's like he knew that this was going to happen. "How do you know that?"

He smiles, and the elevator dings for the floor to the NICU. Walking out of the elevator, he begins to answer. "I provide security to all of the local hospitals. And one of the things that I made sure of for this hospital is that if they do not have the information on the patient, they are escorted off the premises and not allowed back on the grounds until they are added to somebody's list."

Looking at him in awe I ask, "Who are you, and why are you being so nice to me?"

He laughs at me again, and I get a little annoyed with the fact that he keeps laughing at me. "Why do you keep laughing at me? I don't find anything about this amusing. What do you want from me? Nobody does the things that you have done out of the kindness of their heart. Everyone expects something back."

His smile fades into a scowl of perplexity. "Hear me when I say this to you. Just because you have never experienced it doesn't mean it doesn't exist. I don't need or want anything from you in return for any of the gifts that I have given to you. I hate that you were never treated with the love and adoration that you are worthy of. I'm not some fuck boy who is playing games in these streets. I am somebody who doesn't fuck around about anyone that I see. You asked what I want from you, and it's simple. I want to get to know you. Not the version of you that you have to show these men who wonder what you bring to the table, but the you that looks like you did yesterday when I pulled in your driveway at the ass crack of dawn. I'm not asking for your hand in marriage, just your hand in friendship for now."

His words knock the wind out of me, but strangely,

my body wants to submit to this man. "O.. okay. Friendship is all I have to offer right now." My words are a whisper compared to how my body screams for him.

He steps in closer to me as we get to Mina's door, and leaning down, he kisses my forehead before turning to leave. When my stomach growls, it stops him in his tracks. The shit was so loud that I'm embarrassed.

"So, you haven't eaten yet?" he asks, smiling again.

"I didn't have time. I had just woken up when G called, and then you showed up..." I clasp a hand over my mouth to stop the word vomit spilling out everywhere. Why the fuck am I telling him all this shit?

His smile never falters, even with knowing I just said that Giavonni called me this morning. Did he even hear that part, or did he just not give a fuck? "I'll have Maya bring me something to eat when she comes up here," I say, hoping that this will be the end of this conversation. I turn to start washing my hands to go in to see my baby.

"I don't have time to feed you right now, but I will make sure that you get food in the next twenty minutes. And I will see you tonight for dinner." I look up and wish I had a bar of soap to drop on purpose. My smile fades when I see Giavonni appear behind A'Meir.

When A'Meir turns around to see who I'm looking

at, I see the hate in Giavonni's eyes. A'Meir steps in closer to me, handing me napkins to dry my hands and whispers, "Just say the word, and I'll end this before he even gets started."

"Well hello, Mia. You're a hard bitch to catch up with these days, and I see why now. I might have been wrong about Sincere, but I guess my mama was right about you all these years."

A'Meir stiffens beside me at G's words like he caught the blow that was meant for me.

"Giavonni, why are you—" My words cease at the loud crack of A'Meir's fist connecting with Giavonni's mouth. I swallow anything else I was about to say. As Giavonni stumbles backward, I see Cliff climbing off the elevator with two other men.

When Giavonni recovers, he acts like he's ready to charge at A'Meir. But I step in front of him. "You need to leave. You have already taken my son from me, and I be damned if you will take anything else. I hate you. I curse the day that your mammy met your daddy. You want to call me a bitch and accuse me of being a whore when I am the one who paid for the DNA test of three men to figure out which one was your father is nasty work. Treating women the way that you do won't make your daddy love you. You need to know that I could have fucked plenty of niggas, but instead I sat at home waiting on your trifling ass to be the man that I needed. I know now that you are incapable of being a man for anybody because you are a fucking child trapped in a man's body. You want to bring your ass in here and—"

Suddenly, A'Meir pulls me back out of Giavonni's face. "You're better than this, Mia. You don't owe him shit. Stop wasting words on a person that could never understand them," he says to me, brushing the fresh tears from my face. "Let these be the last tears you shed. You are healed even if you don't feel like it right now."

He pulls me in for a hug, and I see Giavonni being pulled in the other direction by one of the men with Cliff. "This shit not over Mia, I'll see you in court. And you bet not have that pussy nigga around my fucking daughter," he shouts as they escort him into the elevator.

"Now, she's his fucking daughter," I scoff as I wash my hands again.

With all the commotion, I wonder where the nurses are. None of them seem to have even looked up while this was unfolding. Something else is going on here, and I'm not sure what it is, but I am grateful we didn't get put out this fucking hospital today. I go in to see my baby girl, and my heart breaks all over again seeing her tiny body lying there fighting just to be here.

I want to scream because after all the shit I have

been through, he wants to come up here right now and make shit worse. My body shakes with anger, and I want to fucking scream. I don't even realize that A'Meir is in the room with me until he wraps me in his arms. My anger melts away with every inhale of his cologne.

God, if this man is your angel just say that.

He holds me just long enough for my body to relax before there's a knock at the door. A'Meir opens the door, and Cliff hands him a black lunch bag. He gives him a pound before closing the door back. "I promised you breakfast. It's nothing crazy though since its short notice. Just an omelet with spinach, mushrooms, onions, tomatoes, sausage, and cheese. There is also some cheese grits and homemade biscuits."

My stomach growls again just at the smell that radiates through the lunch bag. "How?" I ask.

"My mom makes breakfast every morning to feed the crew at my landscaping company, and I had Chris bring some over on her way up here. She'll be in soon to speak to you about Mina, so eat up so you can concentrate when she comes in."

Laughing I say, "If I eat all this, I'm going to be in a coma by the time she gets in here." I head over to the table in the room and begin to unpack the food when my alarm goes off, alerting me that it's time to pump.

Has it really been two hours already?

I blow out an exasperating sigh when I see A'Meir grabbing a pair of gloves before unpacking my breast pump and setting it up. I jump up because what the fuck is happening right now? "I got it," I say, almost knocking the omelet over.

"Sit and eat. This will be here for you when you're ready to use it."

My ass finds the chair at his words, and I begin to feed my face while watching him as he puts my pump together and then writes the dates on the bags that I would use to store the milk. The knock at the door brings me out of the trance that I slipped into while watching this man. Chris opens the door with Maya and two nurses in tow.

Maya takes one look at what's happening in the room before looking at me and mouthing, "Oh. My. God. Marry that nigga."

I almost choke trying not to laugh at her. What the hell is going on? This has got to be the twilight zone.

After Chris finished up with Mina's stats for the day, I felt lighter. My baby girl is now three pounds and starting to learn to suckle, meaning she would be bottle feeding soon. Nothing that had happened before this moment mattered. Chris also asked me questions about how I'm coping with postpartum and how I'm healing. I'm so glad that she was there. She basically saved me and my daughter's life. I feel like I can never repay her for what she gave me.

ON THE RIDE BACK HOME, Maya acts as if she wants to talk but isn't sure how to bring up the topic, so I take it upon myself to make it easier on her. "The wedding was really one of the happiest moments of my life. I was surrounded by everyone that I loved, or so I thought. The week after we had the ceremony, I found out that he was sleeping with three different women the night before the wedding. I was so hurt that I didn't know what to do. I thought that because we were finally getting married that he would stop. I started to tell myself that the incident was just his last hoorah. I was so hurt that at first, I forgot to take the marriage license to the courthouse. When I remembered, I was laying in the bed one night after he was posted on the blogs with one of those trashy IG chicks. I wondered how long I had to turn it in, so I grabbed my laptop and googled it. Simply put, it stated no license, no marriage.

"I panicked at first, so I called my uncle to ask him what I should do. He told me that I could turn it in at any time, but of course then he wanted to know why I hadn't turned it in in the first place. When I told him everything, he just sat there for a minute. He told me to figure out what I wanted to do and stick to my guns. I decided to talk to G about what I found out in hopes that he would stop. He told me it was the last time, and I believed him. For a solid year he was the man I needed him to be. But I know now that was always his way of manipulating me into believing he was being faithful."

By the time I'm done explaining everything to her, we pull into her driveway. "Well, shit. All this time you could have just left?" She looks at me with concern in her eyes.

"Not really. Nobody knows that we aren't married except me, my uncle, and now you. He doesn't even know." We step out the car, and I feel so much lighter with her knowing this. I know she is going to be pissed for me not telling her, but I didn't want anyone to know just in case I decided to turn the license in one day.

"I hear what you are saying, but I don't understand why you didn't just leave. Why stay in something that was hurting you? Especially when you knew I would have your back no matter what." Maya's words were filled with love and concern.

"I went through a time where I believed the things that he was telling me. I thought I really was the problem, so I started working hard on trying to be a better person. When he would tell me I wasn't being a good partner, I would do more to get him to see that I was.

When he cheated, I would try to mimic the women he was cheating with."

She sweeps me up in her arms and I feel the tears start. "You were always worthy of a love that was only for you, and it breaks my heart to hear you say that you thought anything less for yourself. Our whole friendship, I've looked up to you. No matter what the situation, you've always handled it with grace. Do you know what it's like to watch your friend get fucked over and not get revenge or anything? When we went to Vegas and you saw Sincere for the first time in years, I thought for sure you would get your lick back after the way G has been treating you. But the fact that all you did was speak to him and an old classmate then let me get drunk and go back to the room and chill was mind blowing."

Recalling the trip, I smile at how much fun we had on the way there and the bonding moments we shared. We migrate into the living room to continue the conversation when the doorbell chimes. Heading back to the door, Maya opens it.

"Oh, fuck no!" she says, slamming the door back.

"Who was it?"

She holds up her phone, and I laugh at the sight of Sincere standing on her porch.

"Girl how does he know where you live?" I ask while walking down the hall towards my room.

"Nope. No ma'am, bring your butt back here and go tell that man to leave." She follows me to my bedroom, stopping me from entering.

"What am I supposed to do to get this man to leave? I have Amelia working with him and his team on the fundraiser so I don't have to be around him."

Silence falls between us but is quickly erased at the sound of doorbell chiming again. We stare at each other before Maya tilts her head for me to answer the door. I look at her and roll my eyes as I head to the door. "If he kills me just remember it is your fault."

She sucks her teeth as we approach the door. I turn to her, hoping that she won't make me actually speak to Sincere when I have a great idea. I head to the counter where she left her phone and open the Ring app. "Look, he doesn't know that I'm here, so you go to the door and talk to him, and I'll watch just in case I need to get Onyx to lay his ass out."

Onyx is the .380 that I keep tucked in my bra whenever I leave the house. She looks at me and smiles, and I know I'm going to regret whatever she's about to say.

"Fine. But you have to go on a double date with A'Meir after your six weeks postpartum checkup."

My mouth falls open because I just knew that she was going to say something like this. Waving her phone in my face she says, "Tick tock."

I can't stand this girl sometimes, but I can think of

worse things that I would rather be doing. "Fiinnnee," I say as I snatch the phone from her.

Maya skips to the door just as I watch Sincere turn like he's going to leave. I go to stop her, but she gets to the door before I can get to her.

"What do you want, fuck boy number two?" I hear her ask.

I tilt my head back and chuckle because only this girl.

"Nice to see you again, Maya," he says, smiling at her.

"Boy tuck that smile away. It's not making any panties wet over here."

He drops his head, but this time when he looks up, he looks serious. I instantly reach for my gun because, Not Today Satan.

"Okay, on some real shit. Have you talked to Mia? Some shit went down a few weeks ago at my office, and I haven't spoken to her since. I been texting and calling her for weeks now. When I call her office, she doesn't answer, and when we have meetings about the foundation, she always sends Ameila. Is everything okay with her?"

Maya blows out an exasperated sigh. "First, don't come over here playing coy like you don't know what the fuck you did."

His face contorts with wonder, and I can see he is

nervous.

"You ambushed her with information about some shit that you had known for weeks, and instead of being a normal fucking person, you devised a fucking plan and tried to rope her into it."

Sincere goes to speak, but she holds up her hand, cutting him off. "The fact that you would do something like that proves just how much you don't know about her. She would have never done that to you. If you knew your wife was a harlot, you should have left that bitch and then told my friend so that she could have better protected herself from Giavonni. But that is too much like right. For fuck's sake, the bitch's name is Kimber. Her broke ass mama couldn't even afford to put an L-Y on the end of her name. You men get the fuck on my nerves always thinking that you know what's best for everyone when really you are only doing what's best for your fucking selves."

I place the phone down and decide that maybe it is best if I intervene, because I really didn't expect her to go that far. Maya can't stand men who can't do right. One would assume that she has been done dirty by a man or that she didn't have a father in her life, but in actuality she is simply on the side of right.

When I open the door, I shock them both. Maya looks at me, and I watch as the fire in her eyes dies a little.

"Sincere, I think you should go. We don't have anything to talk about. As far as I'm concerned, you are complicit in the bullshit with Giavonni and Kimber."

He shifts from one foot to the next, and I can tell he's uncomfortable. "Can we just talk about this? I'm sorry. I know that I should have handled that better, but I was hoping that once you saw it, I could finally make you mine. That was my plan. For us to leave them both."

I look at Maya to make sure I heard this crazy muthafucka right. "So, you thought that I was going to be with you after you showed me some shit like that? You are about as crazy as the two of them."

I'm at a loss because how the fuck did he think that shit was going to work?

"I think it's time for you to go. Please don't try to contact me again. As far as the fundraiser goes, I'm on maternity leave, so everything will continue to go through Amelia."

The confusion in his eyes gives me all the satisfaction that I need, but his words stun me to silence. "What do you mean, maternity leave? I just saw you three weeks ago, and even now, that body is as childless as I remember."

His words sting as I'm reminded that I'm also grieving my son. "Do me a favor and go to hell. Thanks to you and your fucking news, I went into premature labor with twins, might I add, that I didn't even know I was carrying. And thanks to your news and my lack of knowledge, one of them died. Since the last time I saw you, I've been in fucking purgatory.

"The only one of us that is childless is you. Here is some food for thought. When women love the dick they're getting at home and being treated like they are the only woman in the room, they don't stray. So, if your wife is fucking G, that says more about you than it does about her. She obviously had a plan of her own. The baby that she's carrying was probably supposed to be revenge on me, but looks like now, instead of it affecting me, it backfired on her. She's stuck with that nigga now, and unless you get a paternity test, so are you!"

Turning to go back into the house, I slam the door. When the door opens behind me, I pull my gun, but I see Maya and breathe out a sigh of relief.

"Damn, you was going to shoot the nigga? He's an asshole but not worth shooting."

My heart feels like it's going to beat out of my chest. I can't catch my breath, and I can tell that this is not good. It's been years since the last time I had a panic attack, but I can tell that's what's happening. I sit down and put my head between my knees.

I wince in pain as I remember my stitches are not quite healed all the way. Stretching my legs out, I try to regulate my breathing. Maya grabs my hands and begins to breathe with me. Looking at my friend, I can only cry as I think about everything that has happened in my life in the last three weeks and five days. I have a baby girl, and my fake marriage is now over. But finally, I can breathe easier knowing I am only responsible for me and Mina.

CHAPTER TWELVE

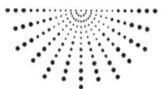

$\mathcal{O}$ver the next few weeks, I settle into my new routine of seeing my baby girl and then going home and working on upcoming projects. Sometimes I find myself in a daze about my baby boy, wondering what my life would be like with the both of them. I know that I'm experiencing baby blues, but that doesn't stop me from going into Mina Joy's room to paint the mural in the nursery. Even after I finish the mural, I keep adding small details because it feels like something is missing, but I can't put my finger on it. It becomes my therapy, since I just don't feel like going to see Dr. Yasmine.

I'm living in a nightmare at times, but it seems like every time I sink into that hole, I remember that I'm not where I started and this isn't the end. Giavonni's plees for me to speak to him fall on deaf ears. I think about changing my number but decide against it. I can't pretend A'Meir's morning inspirational texts don't keep me from even looking twice at the man that once pacified me with empty promises and a gifts forged in lies.

A'Meir's gifts make me uncomfortable at first, and I pray he's done after he gifts me the landscaping of my property which came together quite nicely over the past three weeks. They completely redid my front lawn with beautiful rose bushes that were at a safe enough distance from the house that I could admire them in bloom without the fear of being stung by bees in the spring. I'm completely satisfied with the garden that he placed just off the back of the house. It has all my favorite herbs like basil, coriander, and even a few sprouts of bay leaf plants. There's a divider between my fruits and veggies, and I'm ready to see what surprises he planted there. He truly gifted me with a gift that keeps on giving.

As the weeks tick by, A'Meir continues to let his interest be known. There are food deliveries on days when my favorite shows are on. Then randomly, things that I actually need show up on my doorstep. The most shocking one yet is when I receive a delivery for everything on my Pinterest board for Mina Joy's nursery.

I think that's the end of the surprise until an hour later a team of organizers shows up and organizes the entire nursery. My heart is so full that I call him to thank him.

"Good afternoon, Mr. Frasier," I say when he answers the phone.

"Good afternoon, Ms. Jones."

We start to speak at the same time but he tells me to go first. "I just wanted to call and thank you for the gifts for the nursery. I do feel like it's a bit much though. I feel like I owe you dinner or something," I say, chuckling nervously.

"Don't do that, Mia." His voice shifts into a serious tone.

"Don't do what?" I ask, confused.

"Listen, I'm not going to pretend like Maya hasn't told me some of the things that you went through. But I'm also not going to pretend like I know everything. One thing that I do know is everything that I do for you is because I want to. You don't need to feel like you owe me anything. I'm just showing you how a man that really cares about who you are as a person is willing to bear the burdens with you and take things off your plate that have a solution."

His words are sincere, and I can feel the lump in my throat indicating that I am about to cry. "Okay. I just wanted to say thank you." My voice is softer and the sound of him getting into the car throws me off guard.

"Mia, I'm going to ask you a question, and I want your honest answer."

I mute the phone so that I can let out the sob I'm holding in. Unmuting the phone, I say, "Sure."

"Can I come give you a hug?"

His words shock me a little, because I'm expecting him to ask about my past or ask me something, hell, anything else. I go back and forth in my head. Is it too soon to be allowing somebody in my space? Why am I so attracted to this man? What if he's just like Giavonni?

"Yes," I say before I lose the nerve to say anything else.

He arrives ten minutes later. I gave the guard a set of names allowed to enter the gate, so there's no delay in his prompt arrival. I added him after I realized that he would be here to personally make sure that everything that I asked for with the landscaping was done to his standard.

Now, I think it was just his excuse to see me, and to see him doing manual labor. And God, what a sight to behold. I unlock the door just as he gets to my porch, and moving sideways, I grant him entry into my home. Things have changed since he was last here because I got rid of things that reminded me of my old life with G and replaced them with items that resemble who I am now.

"Would you like something to drink?" I ask, making my way into the foyer.

When he doesn't reply, I notice that he stopped, taking in the changes. He nods his head in approval but doesn't take another step. I walk back over to him a bit confused. Once I'm within arms' reach, he pulls me in.

"I told you, I just needed to give you a hug." He holds my body tightly but gently.

I can't wrap my mind around what's happening. I've never had somebody just hold me. The way he caresses my back as he sways my body makes me emotional. Before I know it, I'm standing in his arms crying, snotting, and barely able to catch my breath. It's like he's helping to heal the parts of me that I didn't even realize were still broken.

As I calm down, he doesn't let me go. Just continues to hold me until my breathing is regulated again. "Sometimes we just need to cry. Our eyes are the windows to our soul, and our tears are the Windex that cleans the windows."

I chuckle a little as I feel his lips on my forehead. My body instantly heats up, and I wonder if he can feel it while his head rests on mine. He shifts to look at his watch, and I can feel that the moment is almost over.

"Can I see the nursery?" he asks.

Shocked, I step back, wiping the last of the tears from my eyes.

"You can see it together. We just finished up," I hear the lead organizer, that I now know is named Jen, say from behind me.

I squeal with excitement as she leads us up the stairs. When we walk into the nursery, I am shocked. Not only have they captured my vision, but there are small details that incorporate baby girl's brother. As much as I hate that Giavonni named our son after him, I love the little G's with halos painted into the mural. He was what was missing this whole time. I cry tears of joy, pain, and excitement all at the same time.

"Looks like mommy and daddy love it. Let's get out of their hair so they can enjoy it."

A'Meir grabs my hand and squeezes gently before I can correct Jen, but when I feel his hand in mine, I don't even want to.

"Thank you so much for bringing my vision to life," I say as I hug Jen and I let her team out.

"It was our pleasure. You're a lucky girl. I can think of a million women who would pay good money to have a piece of a man like that," she says, motioning at A'Meir.

"He's not mine," I whisper to her.

She winks at me before saying, "Does he know that?" Then, she turns to leave without another word.

A'Meir walks over to where I stand, and his cologne makes my pussy jump into his back pocket. If he's not mine, I'm going to need my body to get on the same page with my mind, because these knees are weak. Pulling me in for another hug, A'Meir says, "I'm going to head out, too. I have another meeting, and my dad will kill me if I miss it."

When he lets me go, he walks me back to my door before turning to leave. I watch him pull out of the driveway, and I just want to call him and ask him to stay. Instead, I take out my phone and text.

> Me: Thank you so much for everything. I really needed today.

> BDE: You are welcome and deserving.

The instant reply catches me off guard. I glance down my driveway and see his taillights sitting there.

I clutch my phone to my chest like the girls do in love stories because this is definitely a fairytale.

CHAPTER THIRTEEN

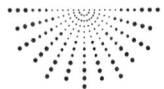

The next day I decide it's a good day to go into the office and make sure that everything is going well and to handle any pressing matters that require a physical signature. I had several projects going on when I went into labor, and my office manager Amelia was more than willing to step in when I told her everything that was going on. Amelia is a good friend from my childhood who I'm also quite close with. I haven't disclosed everything going on because, all that is need to know information, and if you weren't there then you don't need to know.

As she catches me up on the day-to-day lately, we hear the chime of the front door. When I look over, I see Kimber standing in the doorway with a very round belly.

How far along is this bitch?

Ameila jumps up before I can object.

"I'm here to see A'Mia Wallace, please," I hear Kimber say.

It gives me great satisfaction that this isn't my name.

"Do you have an appointment to speak with her?" Amelia asks in a tone matching Kimber's. While Amelia appears to be frail and meek, sis is more vicious than Maya.

"You're her little assistant, didn't you see Giavonni's girlfriend on the schedule?"

Amelia laughs at Kimber's sad attempt to claim G. "Oh, you're the side chick of the week. Congratulations."

Walking into the room, I laugh at Amelia's joke. "How can I help you, Mrs. Cummins?" I ask Kimber, using that to let Amelia know just who this woman is and how chaotic of a shit show this has become. When she looks at me, I can see the shock.

"I just came here to warn you about Giavonni. He has been talking crazy lately and said that he plans on getting you back for taking his daughter from him. At first, I thought he was going crazy, because I didn't know you were pregnant. But when he brought this home and I saw what was inside, I realized what he had done."

She holds out the box to me, and I hesitate to move,

so Amelia grabs the box from her. She peeks inside and closes it back before walking slowly to me with tears in her eyes. She places the box on the desk beside me and opens it, and my heart shatters. Inside, there's a picture of my sleeping son next to his sister, his blanket, footprint card, birth certificate, death certificate, and a small urn in the shape of baby booties. My heart is filled with pain and love all at the same time.

"If there is nothing else, you can leave," Amelia says as she escorts Kimber to the door.

"Wait." I cross the room and wrap Kimber in my arms. "Thank you for the warning, and thank you for bringing my baby back to me."

When I release her, she is in tears. "I'm afraid for you and me. I wanted to hurt you because Sincere has always loved you. He never even attempted to hide it from me, but he always tried to convince me that it was a platonic love." She sniffles before continuing. "I never believed him, so when I found out that Giavonni was your husband, I wanted you to know how it felt to have the person that you love more than anything to not be completely yours. When I got pregnant, he begged me to get an abortion, but I told him that it wasn't his. He didn't believe that the baby was Sincere's though. I have been telling him that when I got pregnant, he wasn't even around, because you two were out of the country for your anniversary."

I realize that she doesn't know that Sincere knows about the affair. I figure since we are sharing truths, I will tell her mine. No need in her going through a surprise divorce. As much as I want to hate her I can't; she just wants what any wife would want. Hell, she wants what I want, to be loved genuinely by the men we devoted our lives to.

"Sincere knows about the affair. He also thinks that this is not his baby, and he has a video of you fucking Giavonni. He showed it to me the day before I went into premature labor." I decide to keep the rest to myself because what good would it do to confirm that this man didn't love her like she always suspected. I'm not willing to kick her while she's down. When my words sink in, she drops her head in defeat. "Just give him the divorce when he asks. You have your practice, so take your money and live your best life."

At my words, she nods and turns to leave. As soon as she exits out the door, the first shot rings out.

MY EARS ARE RINGING, and I can't see clearly because of a pain in my right leg.

What the fuck was that?

When I sit up, I see Kimber. She lies in a puddle of blood. I scream for Amelia, but she doesn't answer. I try to get up but as soon as I start moving, I see the police and firemen coming through the door. Sitting up, I scream for Amelia again, and this time I see her. She's in the corner not moving or responding. I try to get to her, but the police go over to her first. I wait for them to say if she's alive or not.

"I need a medic here," I hear the cop scream as he does chest compressions on Kimber.

"Look at me, can you hear me, ma'am?" I finally begin to pay attention to the paramedic in my face.

"Ye- yes, I can hear you. Is she..." I point to Amelia in the corner.

"She's okay, ma'am. Looks like she may have just hit her head ducking for cover. She doesn't have any injuries."

"Ma'am, do you know who would do something like this?" a fat white cop with what looks like chicken crumbs on his shirt asks me.

"No, I don't. This was my first day back in the office."

He grunts and smirks like he doesn't believe me. "Are you sure? You mean to tell me none of those boys you work with have no gang beef or anything?"

The way his ass said 'boys' makes me want to kick his ass with my bad leg.

"Are you insinuating that this woman's non-profit

was shot at because of the black young men she chooses to help?"

The sound of A'Meir's voice shocks the hell out of me. What is he doing here and how did he even know to come?

Yep, definitely an angel.

The officer's smirk disappears at the sight of A'Meir. "Mr. Fraiser, I wasn't saying that. I was just—"

A'Meir stops him mid-sentence. "You were just leaving to do your fucking job. I'm sure that you would hate for your boss to get a call from my boss about you interrogating victims on the scene of a crime while the paramedics are still trying to treat them."

Paul Blart Jr. walks off, clearly shaking.

"What are you doing here?" I ask as they lift me onto the stretcher.

"I was going to come by to bring you lunch when I saw all the commotion. Maya told me earlier that you were in the office and Amelia was supposed to keep you here until I got here."

I take another look around my office space and realize that the only person who would do something like this is Giavonni. "Can you do me a favor?" I ask A'Meir.

"Anything," he replies.

"Can you make sure Kimber is okay and see that Amelia is okay as well?" He drops his head. The paramedic says they are ready for transport, and he walks through the shattered glass as they roll me out.

"Kimber was already transported. They're trying to save the baby. She was shot in the head."

My heart sinks as I think of that poor baby that won't have a mother, then I remember the shadow box that my son is in. "My son," I shout.

The paramedics stop in their tracks. When I look over my shoulder, I see Amelia walking behind me with the box in her hand. With tears streaming down my face, I silently thank her as she places the box on my lap. A'Meir looks at me with confusion until I open the box. His face softens as I give the paramedics the okay to take me.

"I'll meet you there."

I watch as A'Meir turns to walk away. "Ride with me," I yell behind him.

He jogs back to where I am as they load me up. Taking out his phone, he stares me in the eyes as he climbs in. "Cliff, follow the ambulance, and tell Taj and Liq to find out who did this shit."

We arrive at the hospital, and I can't help but wonder why somebody would do something like this. They rush me back and determine that the bullet passed through my calf muscle without any damage. I'm relieved to say the least. I'm injured but okay, and Amelia is also checked out and is fine.

When A'Meir wheels me out the hospital, we pass a waiting room. I glance over to see Sincere's face. He looks disheveled and lost.

"A'Meir, can you hold on a minute?" He stops in his tracks as I point to where Sincere is seated.

Sincere takes one look at me, and the rage that I see in his eyes scares me. "I'm going to kill him." His voice is deep and sinister.

"We don't know that it was him, Sincere."

He scoffs at me. "Don't be fucking stupid, Mia. You have been running that fucking foundation for years, and this shit has never happened. The cops might be idiotic enough to think it has something to do with those kids, but Kimber had four bullets in her. Four! She was shot twice in the head and two were aimed at her fucking belly. You think what he did to you was fucked up, but at least you are still fucking here. As far as I am concerned, this shit is your fault. You married a fucking murderer. He killed my fucking wife and tried to kill his son."

Sincere goes to stand, and A'Meir intervenes. "I know you hurting, bruh, but unless you want to end up on a slab too, you might want to stay the fuck seated until we leave." The cool calmness of A'Meir's voice chills the room.

"Who the fuck are you? Mia, you got a fucking

bodyguard now? Where the fuck was he when your husband was killing my fucking wife?"

His words sting as flashes of Kimber's body in a pool of blood play in my mind. Instead of responding, I lock eyes with A'Meir. "We can go." It devastates me that it has come to this. Our friendship has ended because of his uncontrollable feelings for me, but I'm to blame. He is no different than Giavonni out here, playing with people's emotions. Kimber's confession about his obsession with me plays with my head.

"I came to offer my condolences to a friend, and to share some things with you, but fuck you. You deserve whatever is coming next. Kimber is only guilty of loving two men that were just alike. Fucking monsters!"

A'Meir turns my chair to leave just as Amelia comes up, being pushed by Cliff. "Oh, by the way. She stopped in my office to give me my son's ashes. It was then that I found out that she still loved you. Through all this shit, she just wanted you to see her like you saw me." My voice breaks at the last word. As tears stream down my face, I continue. "And it isn't Giavonni's son; he is yours."

With that, we leave the hospital, and all I want to do is to get to my daughter.

After checking in on Mina Joy, A'Meir takes me home, and I collapse in my bed after my shower exhausted, but I can't sleep. I toss and turn for what feels like most of the night. Finally, I decide to get up and get some water.

A'Meir scares the shit out of me when I see him leaning against the counter, eating gelato. I glance at the clock, and it reads 3:33 a.m.

"What are you doing up?" he asks with that silky smooth voice.

"I can't sleep. I keep seeing Kimber laying there."

He sets the gelato down while pushing off the counter. He wraps me in his arms, and I can't help but to melt once again. I don't know what it is about this man's arms, but I literally become putty in them. He kisses my forehead as my body melts faster than gelato on a summer day in Georgia. He releases me, and I instantly miss him. Grabbing some water and my pain meds, he follows me towards the stairs.

"How did you even get down here?" he asks. I hop over and go up four stairs with his assistance before sitting on my butt and sliding down, one-by-one. He lets out a laugh that warms my belly. "Let's get you back to bed, Mrs. Scoonchin."

I squeal as he picks me up and carries me up the stairs bridal style. When we reach my bedroom, I kick open the door so that he can lay me back in my bed.

"I'll be downstairs if you need me."

"Can you stay up here with me? Just to keep me company until I doze off."

His dimples make me do involuntary kegels. "Absolutely."

The butterflies in my stomach damn near make me nauseous. I turn on Reasonable Doubt on Hulu, and A'Meir sits on the floor. "You can sit up here, you know."

He gets up and grabs a pillow from the other side of the bed. He comes to my side and elevates my foot before sitting back down at the foot of my bed. "Naw, I'm good right here."

His response catches me off guard. Did I misread the situation? Was I mistaking his gentle qualities for flirting? "Suit yourself," I reply turning starting the show. I can't focus on the show because I'm so annoyed at him not wanting to sit on the bed with me. Pulling out my phone, I text Dr. Yasmine.

Me: What does it mean if a man won't sit in the bed with you but flirts with you all the time?

I'M NOT EXPECTING a reply right now, but when one comes almost immediately, I am grateful.

> Dr. Yasmine: It means that you have established boundaries, and he doesn't want to cross them. If you don't mind me asking, why is your husband on the floor?

I sigh louder than I intend to because I know I have to go speak to her and let her know everything that has happened lately. "

> Me: It's not G, and a lot has happened. Can I come in today after I see my daughter in the hospital?"

> Dr. Yasmine: Daughter? Mia are you okay? Do I need to come to you?

Shit. She doesn't even know I have a baby.

> Me: No, I am fine. Please, can I come in later today? We have a lot to catch up on.

> ...

HER BUBBLES START THEN STOP three times, and then my calendar chimes with an appointment for one o'clock this afternoon. I wait a little longer for a response, but it never comes. When I look up from my phone, A'Meir is staring at me. My face shows that I'm annoyed, but I try to check it before he can notice.

"You know you have Apple TV, right?" He says smirking.

I cover my face, realizing that he saw the texts as they came in. Great, now he's going to think I'm a nut job.

A'Meir climbs in the bed next to me so close that we could share skin. "The reason that I didn't want to get in the bed with you is because I would want to hold you like this." He pulls me in close until we are one. Our lips brush as he continues to speak.

"I would want to do this." He brings my hand to his lips and kisses my ring finger.

"And this." He kisses my shoulder.

"And this." He gently kisses my neck.

"And finally, this." He cups my face and kisses me gently.

I moan into the kiss as he caresses my back, drawing infinity symbols along my spine. When he pulls back, I am mind blown. The lust in his eyes makes me want to go in for another kiss, but when I feel how wet my shirt is, I'm quickly bought back to reality. My boobs have leaked milk due to my arousal. Ashamed, I quickly cover myself and try to hide the growing stain on my shirt. He climbs out of the bed and grabs my breast pump so that I can pump. He comes back over to me, lifting my shirt over my head.

Climbing in bed behind me, he allows me to lean on his chiseled chest. As the pumps begin to draw nutrients from by body, he gently kisses the back of my neck. The sensation of his lips caressing and gently suckling on my neck coupled with the pulling of the breast pump on my sensitive nipples causes me to come undone. There is a puddle in my panties, and I know he can smell my pheromones. I've never experienced a climax like this before, but I can't come down.

His dick is rock hard on my back, and I want it so bad. The mere thought of him putting that dick inside of me makes me come so hard that milk starts to overflow the breast pump. He helps me get cleaned up and holds me while I drift off to sleep.

NEWS ARTICLE

News article

Breaking: Former NFL Star Giavonni Wallace Arrested for Arson

In a shocking turn of events, former NFL wide receiver Giavonni Wallace was arrested on Thursday for allegedly setting his own Scottsdale home on fire. The incident occurred in the early morning hours, with a neighbor reporting the blaze while out walking her dogs.

According to the Scottsdale Police Department, officers and firefighters responded to the scene to find Wallace sitting in his car in front of the burning house. In a stunning display of defiance, Wallace allegedly attempted to prevent the firefighters from extinguishing the flames, leading to his immediate arrest.

Wallace, who played for the Pittsburgh Steelers from 2014-2016 before being traded to the Dallas Cowboys from 2016 to 2021, shared the residence with his wife A'Mia Jones. However, authorities have confirmed that Jones was not home at the time of the incident.

The motive behind Wallace's actions remains unclear. "We are still in the process of investigating and gathering information," said Tatianna Jamison, the spokeswoman for the Scottsdale Police Department. "We cannot speculate on why Mr. Wallace allegedly set the fire at this time."

Wallace has been charged with arson and is currently being held at the Glendale County Jail. His arraignment is scheduled for Tuesday due to the President's Day holiday on Monday.

This is a developing story, and we will provide updates as more information becomes available.

CHAPTER FOURTEEN

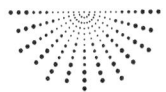

*T*he sound of banging wakes me out of my sleep. I'm still wrapped in A'Meir's arms, and I hate to move. When I hear the banging start again, my phone chimes. I look at my front camera and see Maya, Chris, and.. *Is that the fucking Mayor?* Jumping from the bed, A'Meir stirs.

"What's wrong, Mia?" he says, realizing that I'm trying to make myself presentable.

"I think the mayor is at my door."

He rolls his eyes. "I'll get it, Mia. If my dad is at the door, he's looking for me."

I continue to get dressed when I realize what the hell he just said. "Your dad is the mayor?"

He looks almost ashamed to admit it. "Yes. Now wait here, and I will get the door," he says.

"Fuck no. Maya and Chris are with him," I say skipping past him and attempting to get to the stairs first. The boot on my foot slows me down.

A'Meir stands in front of me at the top of the stairs. "Just get on my back if you going to come." He goes down two stairs, making him short enough for me to get on his back. When we reach the bottom of the stairs, he walks over to the door like he forgets that I'm on his back. He puts me close to the alarm panel so that I can type in my code to the door, and then he opens it. Maya is the first to enter.

"What the hell, Mia? I've been calling you for the past three hours," she says before realizing that A'Meir opened the door.

"Son, what the hell have you gotten yourself wrapped up in this time?" the mayor asks next.

Chris is abnormally quiet, and it kind of scares me. A'Meir walks me over to the couch, gently lowering me down.

Maya is the first to speak. "Have you looked at your phone today?"

"Um, no. You woke me up with your FBI-style banging like you don't have a key."

She blows out a sigh as she starts to tell me what the hell is going on. "Giavonni has been arrested."

I stare at her, waiting for her to say something that is going to matter to me.

"Last night, he burned down the house. He wasn't harmed, but the house is gone."

Looking at her, still my face is expressionless. "Good riddance," I finally say as I attempt to get up from the couch.

"Am I missing something?" Mayor Frasier asks.

"For the past ten years, that man has cheated on me, lied to me, and made me feel less than. Don't take pity on me though, because I'm to blame for not leaving before now. I wasn't strong enough to leave. But with the help of my therapist and all of these recent events, I knew it was time to go."

He looks at me with the same eyes that A'Meir looks at me with. "I see," is all he says before motioning to A'Meir to follow him outside.

"I'll be right back," A'Meir says, leaning down and kissing my forehead.

Maya does a little dance in her seat before Chris clears her throat. "So, when the hell did you start letting strangers put their lips on you?"

I giggle like a schoolgirl as I spill the details of last night.

Chris looks at me with a strange look on her face. "Look, Mia, I like you, but you're a married woman, and all this shit surrounding you is not a good look for my brother. I know you like him, but you need to unload the truck before you go back for another load."

Maya and I look at each other in disbelief. "Chris, I thought you understood my situation, I thought you realized that I am not the problem, but your words are all the confirmation that I need. For your information, I'm not married to Giavonni. I never turned in the marriage certificate. I am free to do whatever I choose with whomever I choose. And right now, I choose for you to get the fuck out of my house, and if your fucking father feels the same way, he can leave too."

I'm seething at her words and her fucking analogy sucked. Her eyes grow big, and Maya agrees with me. "Don't look at me like that. You just said some foul shit without getting the entire story. So now you can leave willingly, or I can make a fucking scene."

Chris face goes from disbelief to hurt. When she walks over to Maya, she's greeted by Maya's hand in her face. "Step," Maya says before flicking her off.

Chris walks outside, and I pick up my phone to listen to what's happening on my Ring camera.

"What are you doing out here?" Mr. Frasier asks.

"I might have overstepped. I'm sorry." I can tell that she's talking to A'Meir, and I wait to hear his response.

"Go wait in the car. I leave you alone for one second and now you've pissed the girl off. She has been through enough. I bet you said some of that judgy shit that your mama would say."

I hear Chris inhale then her feet moving before a car door opens then closes.

"Son, if you're sure about her, then I will have your back. Just make sure that you know what you're doing. That woman has been through things, and you haven't known her long enough to know her triggers. When she needs space, you need to make sure that you give her just that. You don't know if she's ready for what our lives entail, so you have to be sure. Talk to her. Then let me know what decision you make."

I watch as A'Meir hugs his father before heading back into the house.

"Close the app, fool, before he catches us," Maya says snatching my phone.

A'Meir comes back in, and I look up at him, searching for any change in his mood towards me. He hasn't given me any mixed signals, but I'm not sure if he has the same reservations as Chris.

When he enters the room, he immediately begins to apologize. I hold up my hand, unwilling to allow him to clean up a mess he did not make.

"You can't apologize for Chris. You don't even know what you would be apologizing for."

He nods his head in agreement before joining me on the couch. "Do you need help with getting ready to see Mina?" he asks after looking at the time on his phone.

"We need to go to the hospital first. And then I am going to my appointment." Maya looks between the two of us, realizing that we have really gotten closer over the past eight weeks. A'Meir helps me up from the sofa so that I can begin to start my day.

We received great news at the hospital that Mina Joy now feeds from bottles and her weight has stopped fluctuating. In the upcoming days, I will be able to finally bring my baby girl home. The news excites me and I can't wait to settle into a permanent routine that doesn't include the hospital. This has been a long time coming.

On top of that, I'm finally cleared as well. All my stitches have dissolved, and I'm as good as new. As we leave the hospital, I prepare mentally for my talk with Dr. Yasmine. There is so much that I'm going to have to unpack. Before my world spiraled out of control, I met with her every Wednesday. Seeing her weekly helped me tremendously while I was healing from the victimhood mentality. In my sessions over the years, I went from not knowing that I was being abused, to being the victim, to learning to deal with the abuser and make my marriage work.

When we pull into the parking lot, A'Meir and Maya get out of his car. They look like my emotional support animals as they trail behind me when I walk into the office. The smell of jasmine and lavender fills my nostrils as soon as we enter the lobby, and my body instantly relaxes. One of the best things to come out of this is I was able to find all-natural ways to cope with my anxiety through scents. As I inhale, I feel my body relax causing me to realize that I have been wound tight since this shitstorm started in my life. We sit and wait for Dr. Yazmin to become available. When her door opens, I have so many emotions all at once.

"Where would you like to start?" Dr. Yasmine's voice calms me as I lay on her couch.

"I guess at the beginning." By the time I finish explaining everything that has taken place, thirty minutes has passed.

Dr. Yasmine looks at me with eyes of concern. "We have a lot to unpack. But I think we should start with the text messages that you sent me last night. The gentleman in the lobby, is that A'Meir?"

The sound of his name makes me blush a little. "Yes, that is him," I exclaim.

"You seem to like him, it's written all over your face."

I can't help but smile at the thought of everything that he has done for me. "He does make me happy. It's something different about him. Like I don't have any worries when he is around. But I feel like everything with him is moving too fast. Like isn't there a time limit for how long I should wait before I am allowed to be with another man?"

She shifts in her chair, and I recognize that she is about to drop a gem. "Mia, you've been healing for years. Your pain, your fears, even your reservations have all been tackled in our sessions. We spoke about how you would always put Giavonni and his needs before yours. You have been working hard in each session to build yourself back up, and in doing that, you started to detach from things that were hurting you. That included your marital relationship with Giavonni."

I sigh because I know that she's right, but it doesn't change the fact that I may be moving way too fast. "Do you think that it is too soon to be with someone? I mean, everything that I have going on is a lot, but he just makes me feel so..." I have trouble describing the feelings I have been having.

"Secure? Protected? Horny? You have been in a relationship so long without security that you don't even recognize it. You have an irrational fear which causes you to try to protect yourself from something that isn't even happening. I realize now that while inside your marriage you were experiencing what I consider the pedestal effect."

I sit intently, waiting for her to finish.

"The pedestal effect is when you set an expectation for yourself or someone else that is unrealistically attainable. Many times, we see other friendships, relationships, even situationships, and want the life of another. What we don't realize is that many times they are not living the life that we think. They project perfection outwardly so that you can't see the imperfections they are masking. Unknowingly, we begin setting standards in our heads based on what we see someone else requiring for happiness. We watch the gestures and actions of others and don't realize that sometimes those are reactions to impure actions. The higher the pedestal, the harder you fall.

"Example: Will and Jada. The world always said that they wanted a relationship like theirs. But when the world was actually let inside the marriage, you hated the inner workings and could not identify with what you wanted to be a perfect relationship."

"When we meet a person, we quickly come up with a view of what we want them to be in our lives. We almost immediately put them on a pedestal that has not been earned. We quickly relinquish our power out of wanting to believe a person is worthy of many things that they are not. We give trust that has no foundation and are devastated when it falls out of the sky. Everything that we give a person must be earned to come out of this phase. We don't always look at the ideology of what a person's makeup is. We no longer analyze relationships to find if they are even worth pouring yourself into."

"My husband was my savior in my most vulnerable time at a tender and impressionable age of 16. As my first love, I didn't require him to earn any part of my life. I willingly relinquished all of who I was without him even asking. This alone was the reason I lived in hurt so many times. He never asked for my love, support, trust, spirit, or even body. But a certain level of naivety was searching for what was lost, so I quickly attached myself to him and held him to a higher standard than he could even see for himself."

"Making a young man a father when he has yet to learn the true version of himself has caused years of resentment and unnecessary hurt for him and me. Just as he was my first love, he was also my first heartbreak. Years and years, I ignored the signs of who he wanted to be because I had a pedestal that I held him on, without certainty that he could even spread his wings to fly should he fall from grace."

When she had finished speaking, I could see the tears in her eyes. She quickly wiped them away, and I could tell that she was trying to hold it together. I appreciate her sharing a piece of her life with me. All the years that I have been coming to her, I haven't once heard her voice what her life is like.

"I have a question," I start.

"Ask away," she says, looking at me with a glint of curiosity in her eyes.

"Can I bring A'Meir in so that we can speak to him as well? I know that we have two hours today, so I would like to at least find out what his intentions are in a neutral location with a trusted person with an unbiased point of view."

Her smile spreads across her face. "Absolutely. I will go get him." She leaves the room and is gone for about five minutes before returning. After they get settled in, Dr. Yasmine begins. "Why don't you start, Mia?"

I look at her because what the fuck? How was I going to start? She is the therapist. She's supposed to get the ball rolling. "Dr. Yasmine, this is A'Meir. A'Meir, this is my therapist, Dr. Yasmine. I wanted you to join me today because I want to get to know you, but I want to make sure that you like me too. In my past, I have had an issue with setting boundaries."

"My ex was very mentally and verbally abusive towards me. For years, I couldn't tell that he was manipulating me. One day, I was speaking to Maya, and she suggested that I speak to someone. I was diagnosed with relational PTSD. I have done a lot of work on myself, and I am still working to learn and verbalize my triggers."

He grabs my hand, interlocking our fingers. Our

hands touching is the encouragement that I need as he rubs my thumb with his at a perfect pace.

"I am a new mother, and I don't know what I am doing. Both of my parents are dead, but I am prepared to handle this responsibility on my own, especially since G will be in jail for quite a while if he is responsible for Kimber's death. I haven't been in any real relationships besides the one with Giavonni. There was this one guy from your dad's office that I used to flirt with via email, but it was never anything serious. All of this is new to me. I don't want somebody that can't be with one woman. I believe in monogamy and won't tolerate or accept anything else. I understand if after hearing all of this you don't want to date me, but I would love to at least stay friends."

He smiles as I finish what feels like the longest bout of word vomit I have ever experienced. "Is it my turn now?" he asks while waiting for confirmation.

Once Dr. Yasmine gives him the go ahead, he blows my mind. "Thank you for sharing all of that with me. I know that it takes a lot to heal and even more to share your healing journey. I want you to know that I don't plan to ever intentionally hurt you. I can't promise that I will never hurt you because I am human, but I can promise you that I will always work hard to approach everything with love, understanding, and patience. You do have many different things going on in your life right now, but I'm okay with that.

"My dad is the mayor, do you really think I am going to give up on you because you think it's a little tough? Speaking of my father. You mentioned that you were speaking with a gentleman via email." He kisses my hand before continuing. "That man was me. I never use my full name on my emails so that people don't try to bribe me when they realize who I am."

My mouth falls open. I think back to the emails that we exchanged, and while they were mostly professional, there was a period of time that we did flirt in the mornings. It happened during a time G was being very cruel after his injury and I was spending more time out of the home than in the home. It felt good to have someone that wasn't mean to me. But once G started to be kind again, I cut the emails off cold turkey, and I felt so guilty that I told G about them. He laughed it off and said that it was probably a fat bald white guy with an ugly wife. Here I am a year and a half later, sitting next to the man that is nothing like G thought and everything that I imagined.

I look in his eyes and do what I have been wanting to do since he kissed me in my bed last night. I lean in and kiss him. I'm sure it takes him off guard, but he doesn't hesitate to reciprocate.

Dr. Yasmine clears her throat before I get the chance

to deepen the kiss. My phone dings, and my heart sinks a little. I see the news article that Maya has just sent me, but I don't get a chance to read it before my phone rings and I see the hospital's number appear. I hurry to answer, and it's amazing news.

"Ms. Jones, Mina is ready to come home. Dr. Fraiser is going to sign off on her release today."

As much as I hate the things that Chris said to me, I understand where she was coming from. I jump off the couch and do a little dance before sharing the news.

"Let's go get baby girl," A'Meir says.

From Arson to Murder:
Former NFL Star Giavonni Wallace Held Without Bond on Suspected Murder-for-Hire and Homicide Charges

IN A STUNNING ESCALATION of the allegations against him, former NFL wide receiver Giavonni Wallace is now being held without bond on suspicion of murder-for-hire and homicide. The charges come just days after Wallace was arrested for allegedly setting his own Scottsdale home on fire.

According to the Glendale County District Attorney's Office, further investigation into the arson incident led authorities to suspect Wallace of orchestrating a plot to kill his estranged wife, A'Mia Jones. Jones, who moved out of the home, was not present at the time of the fire.

"We uncovered evidence suggesting that Mr. Wallace intended for his wife to meet him at the home, where he planned to take her life," said a spokesperson for the DA's office. "This led us to the disturbing conclusion that he was willing to go to great lengths to harm her."

In a shocking twist, sources close to the investigation have revealed that Wallace was having an affair with Kimber Cummins, the wife of wealthy philanthropist Sincere Cummins. Kimber Cummins was reportedly pregnant at the time of the alleged murder plot, and Wallace believed the child to be his.

"It appears that Cummins and her unborn child were in the way of Wallace being able to reconcile with his wife and may have motivated his actions," said the DA's spokesperson. "We are still investigating all angles, but this certainly provides a possible motive."

Tragically, Kimber Cummins was gunned down last Thursday evening as she exited the office of A'Mia Jones. Authorities have confirmed that Wallace is a prime suspect in her killing. She leaves her grieving husband and son to mourn the loss of her life.

Wallace was re-arraigned on the new charges today

and was denied bail due to the severity of the allegations and the potential threat he poses to his estranged wife and others involved. His attorney continues to decline to comment on the case.

This is a developing story, and we will provide updates as more information becomes available.

CHAPTER FIFTEEN

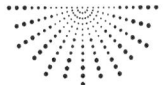

he new charges being brought against Giavonni do nothing but confirm that I never knew the man that I was married to. All this time, I lived with a man that I didn't realize was capable of any of this. As we drive to the hospital, the world seems different. My rose-colored glasses have fallen off, and I can finally see the world for what it is.

The years that we shared flash in my mind. It's like watching our love story unfold. His smile as we played under the covers to the scowl on his face the night he choked me until I passed out. How sweet things started and how right it feels to now be rid of the man that was only guilty of growing into himself.

My hurt shifts to Kimber and her child. She was the real casualty in all of this. All she wanted was love from someone who could never give it to her. You can't get love from another person they've reserved for someone else... in this case, someone he now hated.

The sight of my baby girl snaps my world back into place. When I wanted to be with her father, she was all I wanted, but instead here she is coming to solidify all things right about my decision to leave. My heart swells with love as I am finally able to hold my baby.

She fought to live, and now we get to go home together. She's stayed in the hospital for lung treatments because even though her lungs developed, she still had issues due to the steroid that was given to help them develop. She is truly a fighter.

"She is strong just like her mommy," A'Meir says from behind me.

"Aw you two look so freaking cute," Maya says as she walks back into the room.

Chris follows behind her, stepping up like she is ready to apologize, but I hand Mina over to Maya and hug her. "I know that you were just trying to protect your brother. I understand. I would be doing the same thing," I say as I hold her tight.

She relaxes into me and hugs me tighter. "I'm sorry for everything that you have gone through, and I am glad that you had the strength to not go home. I see a lot of women in here pregnant, and the next thing I know they are being brought in beaten within an inch of their lives. But you are here, she is here, and you both deserve to live and see all the beauty of life," Chris says to me. Maya walks up and we put our arms around her as well.

We arrive home, and I don't want to let Mina out of my sight. Her little smile while she sleeps makes me melt. In the coming weeks, I know that I am going to be super busy keeping her Aunt Maya and my friend Amelia out of my house. Walking into the nursery, I show her the space created just for her. I walk over to the booties I placed on a floating shelf next to the mural in her room.

"Mina Joy, I want you to meet your brother, Giavonni Jacque Wallace. He was nestled next to you while you grew inside my tummy, and I wanted to make sure that you never forget him." Tears stream down my face as I bring my babies back together again.

We settle into a routine over the next few weeks, and Mina seems to be adjusting well to being home. It's a little tough while my leg heals, but everyone is willing to chip in. I generally stay in one part of the house until it's time for us to go upstairs for bed.

Mina loves her baths and that makes bedtimes easier. She sleeps in her room, only waking up to nurse, and for the first few days, she was in the room with me, but it seems like as long as she can smell me she won't sleep. It's hard to not have her nestled next to me, but I know that I'll never get any sleep if we don't make the adjustment. Overall, she's an amazing baby. I know that this is just God smiling on me again.

I don't have as much time to further the relationship that I want to build with A'Meir, but that doesn't stop him from stopping by a few times a week just to check in. Where my time is limited, he makes it a point to show me that he will make the time to come be in our world. I'm always happy to see him because it means that I can take a shower and clean a little. At this point, I think that he comes to see Mina more than me. He comes in, kisses me, and then takes Mina from me. She just smiles and coos at him whenever she sees him. If she is sleeping when he gets here, she'll wake up, and he is the only person that can soothe her.

Waking up this morning, I can feel it's going to be a good day. Amelia stayed last night and allowed me to sleep in, so she was watching Mina. When I get downstairs to my living room, it is eerily quiet. Maya and Amelia stand in the kitchen talking to A'Meir. They stop talking and Maya motions to come stand with them.

"What is going on?" I chuckle nervously, and the looks on their faces let me know that another shoe is about to drop.

"The Defense in Giavonni's case is subpoenaing you

to be a character witness in his trial," A'Meir says, moving towards me.

"Oh, absolutely not. I will *not* be doing that shit. He tried to have me killed and instead he killed his mistress. I don't fucking think they want me to speak to his character." I move past them all and head into the kitchen because my throat is now dry. I thought that after these new charges, I would never have to deal with him again. This nigga just doesn't give up. Why can't he just let me be? I am sick of this shit.

"I think that you should consider doing it. If they want you to be a character witness, you should give them exactly what they're asking for. Don't lie, and don't hold back. Show them who he is. For Kimber and her baby." A'Meir's words are gentle yet understanding.

"You're right. I think I will testify. Lord knows I have a testimony."

He pulls me into his arms and his cologne makes me leak. "Will you go on a date with me?" he asks, putting me back down.

"When?" I ask in return.

"No answering a question with a question." He smirks.

"I will. But you have to let me check with my babysitters to make sure that they're okay with it." I walk back into the living room to find Mina sleeping in Maya's arms.

"Girl, if you don't go get your ass ready for a proper date with that fine ass man before I kick your ass," she whispers.

"Quit cursing around my baby." A'Meir grabs Mina, and the room stops at his revelation.

"I— I mean," he stutters.

"Don't try to backtrack. We know you meant what you said," Amelia pipes up.

I am still stunned into silence. He considers her his? All of this was too much, so without a word, I went upstairs to get myself ready for this date. A'Meir wants to follow behind me, but I hear Maya tell him that he needs to go home and get ready for this fucking date as well.

I hear a smack before I hear Amelia say, "Whatever, you're the cookie eater, heffa."

I laugh to myself because I know that these two are about to go back and forth about the time that Amelia was curious and got turned out by Maya.

I drew a bath to prepare for my date night. It was kind of strange because I used to have a date night routine that called for a day of being pampered, including being waxed, getting my hair done, and picking out a bomb ass outfit that would have my curves being etched in my mind.

I shower before climbing into my bath. My bath is just the right temperature to melt any stress that I was feeling. "Alexa, play some smooth jazz." The smooth sounds of saxophone are just what was missing to bring me a bit of peace. Before I know it, I drift off to sleep.

"Hey, girl." Maya's voice jolts me awake. "Bitch, you still in the tub? A'Meir said eight o'clock, and it's 6:45. And your hair is wet."

I love the fact that my tub comes with a warmer that prevents the bath from getting completely cold, but I curse it right now because I'm gonna be late. "Shoot. Why did y'all let me sleep this long?" I'm annoyed but I check my tone because I know it wasn't their fault.

"Girl, we thought you were up here trimming that coochie, and I assumed you were halfway finished by now. You have been in the tub for three hours now. I climb out, making sure that I don't fall, then fly into my closet to figure out what to wear. When I get in my closet, there is a team in my dressing area, waiting to complete the look. I smile because I know that he has sent help that he didn't even know I needed. I breathe a little lighter as I walk over to start getting myself ready for an amazing night. I rub my body down with my shea butter and coconut oil mix. Next, I grab my personalized Mia J body oil to make sure that my scent lasts all night. After I have on my lace panties with the matching lace bra, I am ready to get dressed.

I walk out to my dressing area and there is now a

hair stylist standing there waiting to get started on my hair.

"Here she is now," Maya announces as I come over and sit in the stylist's chair.

"Hey, A' Mia. My name is Kendra, and I will be doing your hair tonight, and this is my sister Kenice, and she will be doing your makeup at the same time. We know that is a bit unconventional, but this isn't the first time we have had to work simultaneously in a time crunch."

As they get to work, I relax while I listen to the hustle and bustle around me. One of the young ladies does my toes while another is working around the twins to give me a quick manicure. I miss my nails, but they had to go so that I could care for my baby. Forty-five minutes later, I stand in front of a full-length mirror with my natural hair flat-twisted into a bun. It's been so long since I got dressed up to go anywhere, and I look so beautiful. I turn to my team that surrounds me in a circle.

"Bring it in. I am going to have to get your cards so this can be my permanent care team." We all giggle, but that is cut short by the chiming of the doorbell.

Amelia comes in, holding a sleeping Mina, and I kiss her little face and hands. "She will be in Maya's house tonight just in case you decide to let that man come back here and knock them cobwebs off that coochie."

"Are you sure you have everything that y'all will need?"

She rolls her eyes. "If we're missing something, one of us can just run back here and get it, duh."

It was my turn to roll my eyes. Before I could say anything else, Kendra steps back in front of me. "We will get your number, but our services are already paid for the next two years. So, whenever you need us, we will be here. Just let us know," she says as she gives me a final hug.

I look in the mirror at the white bodycon dress and my most comfortable black Jimmy Choo pumps, and I know that I am about to mesmerize this man. The team goes to clean up as I leave the dressing area of my closet. As I get closer to the stairs, my nerves are a mess. When I reach the top of the stairs, I see A'Meir standing at the bottom in a cream sweater with black pants and cream Chelsea boots. He looks delicious, and I can't wait to feel his body against mine.

As I descend, I can feel his eyes peering into me. He reaches for my hand when I'm close enough for him to reach out to help me down the last two steps before leaning in to kiss my forehead.

"I put your flowers in water already." He leads me into the kitchen, and there are four dozen red roses on the counter.

"Why so many?" I ask.

"Because it's time to replace all the flowers in the main areas of the house." His tone is nonchalant. Meanwhile, I didn't even realize he was the one who kept fresh flowers in my house. But when I think about it, when I called to have the delivery set up at my favorite florist, she told me it was already taken care of. I assumed that I had done it while I was getting everything established, but his words provided serene clarity.

"Thank you so much. I didn't even realize."

He smiles as he leads me out of the kitchen and out to his awaiting matte black Lexus LC 500. He opens the door and helps me inside, and I let out the breath that I had been holding. I can't believe I'm going on a date with a grown man for a change. I'm determined to stop comparing A'Meir and Giavonni because it makes me wonder what I ever saw in G. If you know better, then you will do better, and I be damned if this isn't so much better.

CHAPTER SIXTEEN

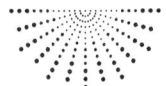

The dinner conversation is light and fun because we're already so comfortable with each other. We're about to order dessert when I get a tap on my shoulder. I turn and Janet stands there, looking like she's the millionaire instead of her son.

"Is this why you can't return my texts? You've moved on to the next man already while my son is suffering?"

A'Meir begins to speak, but I cut him off because it's about time to put this old geezer in her place.

"Look Janet, I think you should leave before you embarrass yourself or get embarrassed."

She rolls her fat neck and sucks her teeth. "I know you think my son is the bad guy in all of this, but I just came over here to make sure that you are going to testify on his behalf. He really needs you right now."

This time I don't stop A'Meir from speaking to her. "She *is* going to testify. As a matter of fact. we were just talking about that, weren't we, love?"

Janet's attitude fades as she turns to address A'Meir. "And who might you be?" she purrs through those big ass veneers in her mouth.

"My name is A'Meir Frasier, and I am Mia's soon-to-be fiancé."

My eyes grow big because what the hell did he just say? Fiancé?

"Well, that won't be anytime soon seeing as she is still married to my son, and I know that he is not going to stand for her being a harlot in these streets."

I'm about to stand when he grabs my hand and shakes his head. "I know that she is married for now. But I am a very patient man. My father taught me to be patient, and my heart's desires will be mine."

At the mention of his father, I chuckle a little, knowing that she doesn't even know who his father is. She scoffs and storms off from the table. We both laugh when she bumps into a server and spills red wine down her cream blouse.

"Let's get out of here," he says, grabbing my hand.

"But we haven't paid yet. And I wanted dessert." I

whine, determined to not let this interaction interfere with tonight.

"We have an open tab here that we pay monthly. This is my dad's best friend's restaurant, so we're good. And I want something that I am sure tastes better than this dessert."

We pull into a driveway twenty minutes later, and my eyes swell with tears. I get out and look at where my old house used to be. So many memories, so much time, all turned to ash.

"I know that you have been through a lot. Seeing this has to be a lot. I think that you have to be here to really be able to let go of what was. And I will work through all of it with you. This place is a physical representation of you. You are a phoenix rising from the ashes of your past. I have never met a woman more beautiful, loving, understanding, and humble. You have been through hell, and now I want to bring you heaven on earth. So, will you be my girlfriend?" His words breathe life into me while I stand in the middle of what should be considered ruins, but is simply a clean slate to build something new. Something that is rooted in love, support, and fun.

I smile while nodding. He picks me up and kisses me softly and ignites my body. I grab his face and deepen the kiss, allowing his hands to grip my ass and the back of my head.

My body trembles with want. I pull back because I can't take the temptation any longer. "I want you inside of me."

He looks down at me pressing me between the hardness of his body and the hardness of his car. I feel how soaked my thong is. Wiggling from between him and the car, I bend over and remove my panties and wave them in his face. He grabs them, placing them in his pocket.

"Hey Siri, Send Chris's Mrs. a text that says Mia won't be home tonight." He looks me in my eyes as Siri alerts him that it is done. We get back into the car and head for his place.

Say Yes by Floetry plays as we drive. He grabs my hand and kisses every finger before he begins to suck on them. I let out a moan because it feels so damn good.

"You aren't playing fair," I say as I pull my hand out of his mouth.

He smiles as we continue to cruise. I'm so hot that I'm going to cum if he hits the brakes too hard. I always had to be tame when it came to sex life with Giavonni. It was dull to say the least. But I remember that this man is nothing like G so I decide to do one of the things that I have always wanted to do.

Pulling up my dress and repositioning myself so my back is against the passenger door, I give A'Meir a full view of my glistening pussy. His reaction is the one I always desired.

"Let me see you play with her," he says while switching lanes.

I lean up just a little and begin to swirl my finger on my clit. I feel my juices leaking onto the seat.

"So fucking wet. Let me taste." I comply and pull my fingers out of my pussy and slide them in his mouth. I almost cum just from watching and feeling him clean my juices off my skin.

We come to a stop, and I realize that we're now in front of a beautiful brick mansion. We pull into the garage, and I begin to close my legs, but he stops me.

"Can I touch you?"

I'm confused why he asks but tell him that he can. I assume he's going to touch my pussy, but instead he guides my dress over my head. I wait for him to continue, but instead he climbs out of the car and comes over to my side. The lights in his garage illuminate with every step. As he reaches my side of the car, I already have my door open. He helps me out, and the faint chill of the night kisses my nipples, making me crave his touch even more. When he pulls me into him for a kiss, I cum just from the oral stimulation of his tongue. My knees go weak, and he wastes no time lifting me off the ground. I wrap my legs around him and the friction of his body as he walks drives me crazy.

"Damn, baby. I can feel how wet you are through my sweater. I can't wait to drink that nectar straight from the fountain."

I lick his neck in response to his words, and his grip on my ass tightens. I know that I should be taking in my surroundings, but I can't even focus right now. The cool chill of the countertop against my ass causes me to open my eyes. He trails kisses down my body stopping at my nipples. He teases them with the lace covering them, gently kneading them with his lips.

Reaching to free me from the last of my clothes, he kisses me, and I can feel the puddle beginning to form under my ass. So much for my fear of vaginal dryness after a hysterectomy. That shit is obviously a myth. He pulls back to take the bra off, and I would normally be against being fully nude, but this man has shown nothing but interest in all of me. I am still a bit insecure about the markings on my stomach where I had surgery.

He lays me back and kisses down my body, studying my reaction to every kiss that he lays on my skin. When he reaches my pussy, his mouth feels like heaven. The heat of his tongue as he slurps on my clit sends chills up my spine. I can feel my body ready to explode.

I try to clamp my legs shut, but he pushes them up

and French kisses my ass before he sucks my clit back into his mouth, sending me over the edge. I cum so hard that I feel like I am levitating off the counter. He doesn't let up and keeps sucking on my sweet spot as I continue to soak his beard and counter.

"Fuck Mia, I could eat you all day," he says while still stroking me with his fingers.

He lifts me off the counter and kisses me gently, and the taste of me mixed with the taste of him makes me want to cum again. He carries me to the stairs and heads up to the top. He continues to kiss me as we walk into his bedroom. His room hosts beautiful tones of deep maroon with gold and black accents. I don't get a chance to take in the room before he lays me gently on the bed.

He removes his sweater, and once again I admire his beautiful sun-kissed skin. The way that his body is chiseled but still soft to the touch blows my mind. *Note to self, find out his exfoliation routine.* I slide back on the bed and begin to swirl my finger around my swollen bud. He watches me as he begins to undress, and I can feel my fingers grow slick from my juices as I watch him.

"Mmmm, A'Meir. I want you so bad. Stop being a tease."

He smiles as he steps out of his pants. His dick is rock hard and the size causes me to pause. He notices my surprise and then pulls down his briefs, revealing the biggest dick I have ever seen in person. I've always considered dicks ugly, but not his. The even skin tone on his long shaft is complimented by a beautiful smooth tip.

"Umm I don't think all of that will fit." I cover my pussy with my hand and close my legs. What was I thinking? This is the first time that I'm about to fuck anyone besides G, and I'm not sure that I'm going to be able to take all that he has to offer.

After putting on a condom, he crawls up the bed to where I wait for him. He spreads my legs and begins to slowly stroke my clit, causing the fire to reignite. He kisses his way back up to my lips until I feel the head of his monster at my entrance. As he begins to inch in, my body trembles.

"Relax, Mia. I got you, baby." He gives me another inch and he pulls back out.

"Fuck, Mia, this shit so tight." Another inch and another retreat.

"You're so wet, baby," he says as he slides back into me. He kisses me deeper while he gives me the last few inches. I feel like he is in my fucking chest. As he begins to move, he deepens the kiss, and I can't help but to wrap my legs around his waist. When he starts with the slow circles, I lose my mind.

"Oh, you feel so good, Meir. Don't stop."

He grunts in response. "This pussy is sucking me back in, baby. You trying to make me cum. I can feel you tightening. Let that shit go. Give me that nut."

He pushes deep, and this has to be what they mean by hitting the bottom. Leaning up, he folds my legs by my ears and begins to slam into me.

"Fuck, daddy, yes, give me that dick," I scream, trying not to tap out.

"I'm about to cum in this tight pussy, baby."

The stars behind my eyes burst, and I cum so hard that when he pulls out, I squirt all the way up to his neck. "Fuck, that shit so sexy. Wet me up baby."

As my walls continue to contract, I can feel when his body grows rigid, ready to release. I start squeezing more as he picks up the pace, signaling that he is near his peak. I pull him in deep, and he explodes. As he comes down, his body jerks a little, and he pulls out and kisses my forehead before he heads to the bathroom to discard the condom. I hear the shower start, and I'm surprised. I've never had someone tend to my after-sex care, so when he comes in the room and scoops me up, I can only giggle. In the bathroom, I find a walk-in shower big enough to fit four people.

"Am I missing anything?" he says, pointing to the counter where all my favorite body care essentials are laid out.

"No. Wait. Yes, I need a—"

He holds up a bonnet and shower cap, and I immediately start smiling. This man has to be sent by God. "Come on now, you know I got you," he says, putting the bonnet on my head before securing the shower cap around it.

Pulling me into the shower, he washes my entire body, even switching to a new cloth to wash my sensitive areas with the Honey Pot cucumber intimate wash. Next, he exfoliates my body, and I feel like he scrubs every man that I have ever been with away. He kneels in front of me with a set of exfoliating gloves and puts one of my legs on his shoulder.

The euphoria of what is happening makes it harder to be shy. Gently, he scrubs my waxed areas before rinsing them with cooler water. I thought he was done until he gets back down on his knees with my pussy in his mouth once again. As he sucks my soul out through my vagina, I can barely see straight.

"Wait, Meir. I, uhhh, God, this feels so good," I say, trying to reciprocate and fuck his face.

"Mmmmmmm," he hums into my pussy, and the low vibrations of his baritone are the catalyst to the explosion that makes him hoist both my legs on his shoulders while he eats me until I pass out.

"Say wake up, mommy," I hear A'Meir say.

I open my eyes to find him fully dressed, holding Mina in his arms. Smiling, I sit up, and then I realize that I am in his house and so is my daughter. Panic sets in, and he must see it in my face.

"Relax. Maya and Chris are downstairs. She said every morning, the first thing you do is check on Ms. Mina, so I told them to just come over for breakfast. I just finished cooking and thought now would be a good time to bring her up to see you. I figured you didn't want Maya all in your business, so I offered to wake you up."

My heart settles, and I can see the concern in his face. "Thank you so much. I'm just not used to this." I reach to grab Mina, but he steps back. "Give me my baby Meir," I say a little louder than I intended.

The look on his face goes from concern to hurt. He hands me Mina and then starts for the door. "I was going to tell you that you needed to change shirts. You're leaking, and I know that even though she just ate, she's going to smell your milk and you're going to wet up her clothes."

Before I can say anything else, he walks out of the room. There's a fresh stack of clothes in the bathroom when I get in there with Mina. While I brush my teeth, Maya comes in looking annoyed.

"What the fuck did you say to that man?" she asks, taking Mina out of my arms.

"Nothing. He was holding Mina, and when I reached for her, he stepped back, and before I gave him a chance to say anything else, I snapped a little and yelled at him to give me my baby."

"Bitch, are you crazy? A'Meir would never do anything to hurt you and especially never do anything to Mina."

I sit on the toilet after finishing my hygiene. "I know. I just had a moment. G would hold things I wanted hostage until I did what he wanted me to do. It started with a purse, then with my first car. I'm just trying to rid myself of all the damage, but my triggers come out of nowhere sometimes."

I know Maya understands, but she is not about to show me any sympathy. "Listen, that man has been through his own trauma, and I don't know the details of his story, just like I didn't tell him the details of yours. What I do know is that you need to quit pushing that man away before I whip your ass. That's a good man, Savannah."

While her words are serious, I can't help but laugh at her reference to *Waiting to Exhale*. "I know, Maya, and I'm trying. Shit, you would think with the dick he gave me last night, I would be more in love than to compare him to anyone else."

I cover my mouth with my hands at my admission. Not only did I tell her that I got my boots knocked, but I also told her that I love him. *Shit.* I'm never going to live this moment down.

Smiling, she walks out of the bathroom. "Told you she loves you," she says to A 'Meir who just walked back into the room. I cover the mortified look on my face and shut the bathroom door and lock it before he can get to it. The tears start to roll down my face and I am filled with embarrassment.

"Mia, you don't have anything to be ashamed of. Come out so we can talk about this." His voice is soft through the door, and I know that I can't avoid him. For God's sake, I'm standing in his bathroom, in his house, across town. There's literally nowhere to run. Twenty minutes go by as I pump, dress, then make sure my eyes are not too puffy.

He pulls me into his arms as I walk out of the bathroom, hugging me so tight that I almost drop the breast milk in my hands.

"I love you too, Mia. But I know you're not fully ready for everything that comes with it. That's why we're taking things as slow as you need to." Kissing my forehead before releasing me, he looks me in my eyes, and I can see the care and love mix.

"Tonight, when you're at my house spending the night, we're going to have a serious conversation. There are things unspoken that I think we need to talk about."

He looks surprised. "Are you asking me to spend the night?"

I giggle before telling him, "No. I'm telling you that

you're staying with your girlfriend and your baby best friend Mina tonight."

I step out of his grasp and head out of the room. At least I thought I did, but I end up in the closet.

"Um, I think you were looking for that door." He chuckles as he points me in the right direction. "Well, last night, I didn't see much of anything but you, so I think you should lead the way since it's your fault I have no idea where I am."

He takes the milk from me, and I follow him out of the room. I must have really been in a lust haze last night because I don't remember any of the things in his house. The interior of the house is amazing. The brown tones are warm with soft undertones of cream, making the house feel like a warm hug. As he leads me down the hallway, I continue to be amazed by the décor. The hallways lead to an opening to two staircases. One looks like it leads into the living room, and the other, the kitchen.

We take the staircase that leads to the kitchen, and I begin to recognize the things that I caught brief glimpses of the night before. I see a massive spread of breakfast laid out on the island. "That looks familiar." I smile at Maya as I walk in.

Her eyebrows scrunch in confusion. Mina is in her bouncer on a floating island, smiling at Chris who's playing peek-a-boo. A'Meir smiles and smacks my ass before going over to offer me a plate.

"Would you like me to fix you a plate?" I ask, attempting to grab the plate from him.

"No, I'll be fixing your plate. You just need to relax. You have a long day ahead of you."

At first, his words confuse me, but then I remember that I have to go to court today. He successfully took my mind off what I have to do today. "What time do we have to be there? Wait, what time is it?" I look around the room for a clock.

Maya slides me my phone, and I'm surprised that it's only 9:00 a.m. I'm not supposed to appear until after lunch. The trial has been going on for a week now, and I'd done my best to stay off social media and not watch anything that would accidentally show me what's going on. I even went as far as to upgrade all my subscriptions so that I won't get any commercials that might have "Breaking News" moments.

A'Meir hands me a plate with some avocado toast bacon and tomatoes.

"You know you don't have to eat healthy this morning. You can cheat today," A' Meir says, looking down at my plate.

I smile, running my hand up his shirt then back down his abs. "I don't cheat, but you're welcome to eat whatever you like. I'm sure your metabolism wouldn't mind."

He picks me up, and I almost drop my plate. He grabs it and sits me on the counter and begins feeding me the toast. Every time I bite one side, he bites the other. Before I know it, we have an empty plate, and now I'm hungry for something else. He must feel the heat coming from between my legs and smiles. Kissing me on the nose, he says, "Later, beautiful. We have to get you home so that you can get dressed."

"You mean to tell me that you don't have a closet for Mina and me here already?" Jokingly, I laugh.

"Wouldn't that be too soon? I mean, I want you both to feel comfortable while you're here, but I thought you would think that was weird if I did that."

Maya cackled. "I told you that his ass was whipped. Hadn't even smelled the girl thong and wanted to make space for her everywhere in his life. Pay the Piper."

Chris walks over and hands Maya 3 crisp blue faces. I cover my mouth, trying not to laugh while A'Meir puts his head down chuckling.

"Let's get you home," he says, pulling me off the counter.

CHAPTER SEVENTEEN

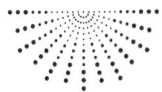

"*A*ll rise, the honorable Judge Osborne presiding."

We all stand as the judge walks in and sits before instructing the room. "You may be seated."

I'm surprised to see a sister sitting as the judge in this case. I'm sure that Janet would have done anything to get her son in front of a judge that could be bought. I look around the court room at all the spectators when my eyes lock with Sincere's. I haven't seen him since that day in the hospital when he looked at me with venom. I hear the coos of a baby and realize that he is holding a beautiful little boy who resembles Giavonni.

I compose myself because I know what Kimber told me, but could that have just been a mix up on the timeline on her part? It had to be if I'm sitting here seeing a baby with the same nose and deep hazel eyes as G.

"Before our break for lunch, we heard from the victim's husband, Mr. Cummins. We will now hear from Mr. Wallace's wife, Mrs. Wallace. Are you present in the court room?"

I stand and wait for the bailiff to lead me to the witness stand. After I am sworn in the torture begins.

MR. BRIGGS: Mrs. Wallace, how long have you been married to Mr. Wallace?

MRS. WALLACE: We had a ceremony on May 23rd, 2012.

MR. BRIGGS: And were you happy during your marriage to Mr. Wallace?

MRS. WALLACE: On and off.

MR. BRIGGS: When you say on and off, are you referring to normal woes that are felt in a marriage?

MRS. WALLACE: What do you mean?

MR. BRIGGS: Were the off times over things as simple as Mr. Wallace not taking out the trash?

MRS. WALLACE: No, he never had to take out the trash in his life, not even as a boy. I am referring to all the times that Mr. Wallace was unfaithful.

[Courtroom murmurs]

MR. BRIGGS: Are you saying that you were aware of Mr. Wallace's past infidelities?

MRS. WALLACE: Yes, I am.

MR. BRIGGS: And you still stayed with him?

MRS. WALLACE: Yes, I did.

MR. BRIGGS: So, there is no reason for us to assume that Mr. Wallace would fear you leaving him if you found out that he was cheating with Mrs. Cummins. I mean you never indicated leaving prior to this incident.

MR. ROBINSON: Objection, testifying.

THE COURT: Sustained. Watch it, Mr. Briggs.

MR. BRIGGS: I'm sorry, your honor. Nothing further.

DIRECT EXAMINATION BY MR. ROBINSON

MR. ROBINSON: Good morning, Mrs. Wallace. Or do you prefer Ms. Jones?

MRS. WALLACE: Good morning, Ms. Jones is fine.

[Courtroom murmurs]

MR. ROBINSON: You testified that you had a ceremony with Mr. Wallace in May of 2012, correct?

MRS. WALLACE: That is correct.

MR. ROBINSON: Can you tell me about that day?

MRS. WALLACE: We had a beautiful destination

wedding in Dubai. We only had our family and close friends. I can still feel the sun on my face. It was one of the most amazing days of my life.

MR. ROBINSON: Were you happy to be with Mr. Wallace?

MRS. WALLACE: At the time, yes.

MR. ROBINSON: When did you decide that you didn't want to be with Mr. Wallace anymore?

MRS. WALLACE: It was after I found out that he was sleeping with Kimber Cummins.

MR. ROBINSON: You said that you have stayed before when there was infidelity. Why was this time different?

MRS. WALLACE: This time it was the wife of one of my friends. And she was pregnant.

MR. ROBINSON: So you knew Kimber before all of this?

MRS. WALLACE: I had only been around her a few times, but all around she seemed nice.

MR. ROBINSON: And you were one of the last people to speak with Mrs. Cummins, yes?

MRS. WALLACE: I was.

MR. ROBINSON: Ms. Jones, have you ever known Mr. Wallace to be violent?

MRS. WALLACE: There was one time we had just come back from a party, and he was intoxicated. He was upset that I didn't let him drive. We argued all the way home, and I thought that it would be the end of it. He still wanted to argue, and I was tired, so I flipped him off and walked away. He grabbed me by my hair and pulled me back into the living room and began choking me. I begged for him to stop, but I passed out before he did. When I regained consciousness, he was on the couch, watching the highlights of the game like I wasn't even there. The next day, when I approached him about it, he told me he didn't remember doing that. He told me he would stop drinking and that he would never do it again.

MR. BRIGGS: Objection, your honor, he is leading the witness. This is to establish the character of my client not to go through all the marital issues.

MR. ROBINSON: Your honor, Ms. Jones is doing just that. She is only testifying to the character of Mr. Wallace.

MR. BRIGGS: May we approach your honor?

THE COURT: You may.

MR. BRIGGS: We would ask that you strike the testimony of Mrs. Wallace. She sat here under the pretense of being married to my client and according to this courthouse there was never a marriage license filed.

THE COURT: Well, counselor, that would be your fault, seeing that you called this witness. You don't get to move to remove her testimony because it does not go in favor of your client. Married or not, this woman has been with this man longer than you have been his attorney, and her testimony will stand. You may continue, Mr. Robinson.

MR. ROBINSON: I'm sorry about that, Ms. Jones. Can you please answer, did Mr. Wallace ever put his hands on you in a harmful way again?

MRS. WALLACE: No, he didn't.

MR. ROBINSON: You said that you were one of the last people to speak with Ms. Cummins. Can you tell me what she said to you that day in your office?

MRS. WALLACE: She said she was coming to warn me. She said that he was talking crazy about getting me back for taking his daughter. She told me that the baby that she was carrying wasn't Giavonni's, she then returned my son's ashes to me which Mr. Wallace had taken possession of.

MR. ROBINSON: What do you mean?

MRS. WALLACE: The day after I found out about Mr. Wallace and Mrs. Cummins, I went into premature labor with twins that I didn't know I was carrying. I lost my son that day, but I also died. When I woke up the next day and the doctors came to speak with me, Mr. Wallace got irate when he realized I never changed my last name. He then gave the funeral home permission to cremate my son before I ever got a chance to hold him.

That's why Kimber came that day. She was returning my son's ashes to me.

MR. ROBINSON: I'm deeply saddened by your loss, Ms. Jones. Do you need a minute?

MRS. WALLACE: No, we can continue.

MR. ROBINSON: Why didn't you ever change your name?

MRS. WALLACE: Because I never turned in our marriage certificate.

[Courtroom uproar]

THE COURT: Order, we will have order in my courtroom. Any more outbursts like that, and I will clear the gallery! Please proceed, Mr. Robinson.

MR. ROBINSON: So technically you are not married to Mr. Wallace?

MRS. WALLACE: No, I am not.

MR. ROBINSON: So, you have nothing to gain here today by testifying.

MRS. WALLACE: No, I came because Kimber deserves justice, and if he is guilty of what they say, then he deserves whatever sentence he is handed. There is a child without a mother right now because of his alleged actions.

MR. ROBINSON: I have nothing further, your honor.

MR. BRIGGS: May I follow up question, please, your honor?

THE COURT: You get one.

MR. BRIGGS: Ms. Jones, is it? Did my client know that you never turned in your marriage license?

MRS. WALLACE: Not at first but he did before any of his legal issues.

MR. BRIGGS: He did?

MRS. WALLACE: Yes.

MR. BRIGGS: How?

MRS. WALLACE: I sent him a text message after I met someone letting him know that I didn't blame him for any of the things that he did while we were together. And that there was no need to get a divorce because we were never married. I explained how when I was going to turn in the license I kept finding out about the different women.

MR. BRIGGS: How do you know that Mr. Wallace saw your text message?

MRS. WALLACE: He keeps his read receipts on. Then he started typing, but the reply never came through.

MR. BRIGGS: Are you currently seeing someone, Ms. Jones?

MRS. WALLACE: Yes, I am.

MR. BRIGGS: If Mr. Wallace did all these things to

you, why would you be able to be in another relationship so soon?

MRS. WALLACE: Because I started healing from the hurt that I endured at the hands of Mr. Wallace years ago. It's like when you have an old car, and you hear the clanking under the hood and you know one day it is going to go out. But instead of buying a new one immediately, you get your credit right, you research the safest cars, and you might even go test drive a new car. But you don't buy the new car until your car finally puts you down. We all deserve a car that we don't have to worry about if or when it is going to put us down. One day your mind leaves and then the heart follows.

[Courtroom murmurs]

MR. BRIGGS: Nothing further, your honor.

THE COURT: Ms. Jones, thank you for your testimony. I am sorry for the loss of your son, and I pray for the healing of your heart. You may step down.

As I HEAD BACK to my seat, Giavonni mouths that he is sorry as he sits there looking like a shadow of himself. Sincere looks at me, and the warmth in his smile lets me know that he approves.

"You did a good job in there," A'Meir says opening my door for me.

"I wanted to help Kimber while not perjuring myself."

He climbs in the car and grabs my hand and kisses it. We head back to my home, and I can't wait to hold my baby girl and take a nap. I must have dozed off in the car, because before I know it, we're in my driveway and A'Meir opens my door to wake me up.

"Somebody is tired I guess," he says, picking me up.

"Absolutely. I had a long night." He kisses me, and I wiggle out his arms. "I can walk sir."

We walk into the house to find Mina sleeping in her bassinet next to the couch. The sight of her makes my boobs grow tight. I head upstairs to change my clothes so that I can go back downstairs to sleep next to my baby. But after I get out of the shower, I see her portable crib next to my bed with her still sound asleep and A'Meir coming back into the room with sandwiches and ginger ale.

"Did you make me one?" I ask, crawling in bed.

"Both are for you. I made you two because I know you didn't eat that much this morning. Avocado BLT." He presents the plate, and my mouth waters at the same time that my stomach growls. I want to eat with some class, but the lime mayo is just too damn good.

"Dang, girl. Breathe," Maya says, interrupting my second sandwich.

I take that time to drink some of the ice-cold Canada Dry sitting on my bedside table.

"You, okay?" The worry in her voice reminds me of the day's events.

"Yeah, I'm good. I feel lighter."

She rolls her eyes. "Can you just give me a toxic answer just once in your life?" she huffs.

"I hope they send his punk ass to jail for what he did to Kimber."

Maya starts to say something but just smiles instead.

"Turn on the TV," Chris says, flying in the room.

Maya grabs the remote, and as soon as the TV comes on, we see the chaos that ensued at the courthouse after we left.

ANCHOR: Dramatic testimony today in the trial of Giavonni Wallace, the wealthy businessman accused of murdering his pregnant mistress, Kimber Cummins. Our courtroom reporter, Michelle Gladsky, is live in the courtroom with the latest.

LIVE REPORT

REPORTER: Tonya, the courtroom was stunned today as Wallace's longtime partner, Ms. Jones, took the stand. She revealed that she and Wallace were never legally married, despite her use of his last name and her previous testimony about their marital history.

Ms. Jones painted a picture of a tumultuous relationship, marked by Wallace's repeated infidelities. She claimed to have stayed with him despite his cheating in the past, but said she decided to leave him after discovering his affair with Cummins, who was a friend's wife and pregnant at the time.

In an emotional testimony, Ms. Jones described losing a son in premature labor after discovering Wallace's infidelity, and how Wallace had her son's ashes cremated without her consent. She said Cummins had returned the ashes when she came to warn Ms. Jones about Wallace's threats.

The defense challenged Ms. Jones' credibility, pointing out that she had no reason to fear Wallace would leave her over his infidelity with Cummins, given her past tolerance of his cheating. But Ms. Jones insisted she was testifying to ensure justice for Cummins and her unborn child.

The most shocking revelation came when Ms. Jones admitted she had never filed their marriage license, meaning she and Wallace were never legally married. Despite this, she said Wallace knew about the license and her reasons for never filing it.

Under cross-examination, Ms. Jones acknowledged

being in a new relationship, prompting the defense to question how she could move on so quickly. She responded by comparing her healing process to responsibly replacing an unreliable car, saying everyone deserves a relationship they don't have to worry about.

OUTRO

REPORTER: Tonya, this bombshell testimony has thrown the case into disarray. The defense is reeling from their own witness undermining their case. The prosecution, meanwhile, is likely to argue that Ms. Jones' revelations further illustrate Wallace's motive to kill Cummins out of rage and fear of being exposed. This trial just took a dramatic and unexpected turn. Wallace's supporters have begun to protest outside of the courthouse for him to be freed.

ANCHOR: Michelle, thank you for that report. We'll continue to follow this case and bring you updates as more information becomes available.

CHAPTER EIGHTEEN

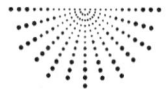

$\mathcal{I}$ wake up to the grunts of my little Mina waking up hungry. I can feel the heaviness in my boobs and know that I'm still going to need to pump after she eats. While she nurses, I pull up my phone and finally start going through my social media accounts. My DMs on Instagram are popping, but after reading a few that say that I was only with Giavonni for the money, I close the app.

After she finishes eating, I change her diaper and head downstairs. I hear laughter so I decide to join in on the fun.

"My baby is up," Amelia says while grabbing Mina from my arms.

"Girl, bye. We all know I'm her favorite," Maya exclaims.

I laugh at the two of them as I follow my nose to the smell of food cooking in the kitchen. I find A'Meir at my stove, making shrimp, beef, and chicken tacos. They all look so good that I decide right then that I'm eating all of them tonight. I walk up behind him and wrap my arms around his waist and lay my head on his back. He lifts my hand and kisses it before putting down the knife I didn't realize he was holding and taking me into his arms.

"How did you sleep, baby?" His tone is light and playful.

"Hard." I lay my head on his chest so that he can hold me. "Did you take a nap too?" I ask curiously. When I fell asleep he was holding me, but I woke up alone.

"Naw, I just waited until you started to snore then I eased out of the bed."

I smack his arm. "I do not snore."

He laughs while dodging my next hit. "You do, but it's cute though. You sound like a baby pig."

I start to chase him, because *no the hell he didn't*. I chase him up the stairs into my bedroom where he grabs me and falls onto the bed. "Do you want to talk about today?" he asks while kissing my forehead.

I assume he means the trial. "No, I'm sick of thinking about G."

He stops me before I start to rant. "I mean about this morning with Mina."

I grow silent because I know we need to talk, but I just hoped it wouldn't be tonight. "It was a trigger for me," I say.

"I know. I heard you speaking to Maya. But I think that because you don't know about me, you still feel like you can't trust me fully."

I nod my head in agreement.

"Let's fix that. Ask me anything that you want to know, and I will answer honestly."

I look at him for a minute before giving in and asking my first question. "Why me?"

He chuckles. "Because I have never met anyone like you. You are smart, giving, loving, nurturing, funny, responsible, reliable, and beautiful. Next question."

His answer makes me smile. "What do you want out of this... relationship?"

He rolls his eyes. "You, duh. And yes, this is a relationship. Next question."

Since he wants to be a smart ass, I decide to take the heat off me all together. "Why are you single?"

His breath catches, and I realize that I caught him off guard with the question. "I was married. My wife, Emmerson, was pregnant with our second child. Everything was fine. She was healthy and so was the baby. I was helping my dad with his campaign for re-election, so I was on the road a lot. I checked in on her and our oldest daughter, Emmi, when I wasn't home, and I even had Chris going by to check in everyday when I was away.

"When she had our son, Taj, she changed. She was irritable and didn't really have a desire to bond with Emmi or Taj. I decided to work from home on the campaign background for my dad. We got her in to see a psychologist who confirmed she had dissociative identity disorder. We got her on medication and into counseling regularly, and that seemed to help.

"One day, she told me she was taking the kids to the park. It was a beautiful day, so I told her I would join her. She insisted I stay at home and finish up work and we could watch Moana together that night. I called her after an hour, and she didn't answer. I texted and still nothing. I started to get worried, so I decided to go look for her. I didn't make it out of the neighborhood before I heard the sirens. She had driven up the wrong side of the highway and collided with seven other cars before she came to a stop. She killed eleven people that day, including herself and our children."

His face is covered in tears as he tells me the story. My heart breaks for him. It makes sense now why he's so hands on when it comes to Mina and me. "I'm so sorry, baby. I hope that you know that you are not to blame. I know that my life is triggering for you, but I am not her. I promise that I'm okay. I just need you to be strong in the things where I'm weak. Like changing tires because I can't jack a car up for nothing."

We giggle at my last comment, and I hold him until our heartbeats are in sync. My stomach growls, killing the moment.

"Well, I guess I need to feed you now."

I giggle as he untangles our bodies. We have an amazing fun night, and I smile until my face hurts.

THE NEXT MORNING, Maya comes into my room and wakes me up. Mina is still sleeping, so I try to be quiet as I figure out what she could want. When we get to the hallway, she hands me a mug of tea. This girl can't even fix tea, so I wonder what the hell is going on.

"The police are here."

My eyes grow big. "What do they want?"

She looks at me. "Bitch, I don't know. I was hoping you could tell me. Have you done anything illegal lately?"

I think for a minute as my door opens, and A'Meir's shirtless body is the only thing I see when I turn around. "The police are here, and Maya is interrogating me about why."

He nods his head. "I know. You need to go down

and talk to them. My dad just called to make sure I was here with you." The worried look on his face lets me know that this is a serious matter.

We all head downstairs after grabbing Mina. I get into the living room and see two uniformed police officers in my foyer. "You wanted to see me?" I say, walking up.

"Ms. A'Mia Jones?" the sergeant asks me.

"Yes that's me," I say.

"We regret to inform you that Mr. Giavonni Wallace was found hanging in his cell this morning."

The words don't sink in at first. "Thanks for letting me know. But why are you telling me? He has a mother you should probably notify."

The officer holds out a letter to me. "He had you listed as his next of kin. You were the only person that he had on any of his paperwork. If he has a mother, you may want to call her before the media runs their report in an hour. We found this letter in his cell."

I take the letter from him as I let them out of my house. The lock doesn't click before I break down in tears. How the fuck did this happen? A'Meir comes and picks me up, and I can only sob. I hate what we'd been through, but never did I think that he would take his own life.

"I have to call Janet," I manage to say. Maya hands me my phone and before I can dial her, she's calling me.

"Hello?" I say through gasps for air.

"Is it true? Is my baby dead?" She is hysterical.

"Yes ma'am. I'm so sorry. I never meant for this to happen."

Before I could finish, she screams, "You bitch! You did this. This is your fault. You lied on that stand and made my baby kill himself. You stupid bitch." As she continues to scream at me, Maya takes the phone out of my hand and disconnects the call.

The next few days are silent in my house. The whispers can be heard, but all I want to do is sleep. Every time I close my eyes, the good times are all that play behind my eyelids. The times that we would go on dates that we couldn't afford so we would dine and dash. The days that I had heavy periods and him bringing me diapers to my door because that was the only way that I didn't mess up my bed.

Maya keeps coming in to check on me, but I can't do anything. It was like because I didn't hate him, the love that I had surfaced. Every night, I cried on A'Meir's chest, and he understood. His connection with death allowed him to be able to separate my love for him from the love that I once shared with Giavonni. His kisses warmed and soothed me.

I know that I'll have to plan the funeral because I'm still on all the insurance policies that he had. I get up four days after the death notification and finally start the planning process. After getting all the arrangements made, I call Janet. The call goes to voicemail, so I hang up and send a text.

"Call me about funeral arrangements. He already had everything written out that he wanted. I just want you to know the info in case you want to change anything."

I call her back after seeing she read the text but she didn't answer. I decide to leave well enough alone and prepare myself to mentally deal with what was to come next. After trying to get in contact a few more times with Janet, I finally give up and text her the date and time of the funeral.

The bubbles turn green, letting me know that she blocked me. I'm okay with that. Her loss.

On the day of the funeral, I have all of the family meet at the funeral home. A funeral car picks me up from my house, and I also have one sent to Janet's home should she want to attend. Maya, Mina, and Chris sit in the middle seat while Amelia, A'Meir, and I sit in the back.

"Are you sure you are okay with this?" I ask him before we pull off.

"I would never let you walk through this alone. I know that you loved this man. And even though she doesn't know him, that was still Mina's dad."

Tears well in my eyes, and I try to fan them away.

I'm grateful for my black sunglasses and my black veil over my face.

The service is long but heartfelt, and the outpouring of fans that came to show him love makes my heart happy. It isn't until we're leaving that I see Janet. She's sitting with her family instead of in front with us. Her face is buried in her nephew's shoulder as we walk behind the casket. I ask them to stop and motion for both of them to join us.

This is the last time seeing her son and the first time seeing Mina. When she sees my baby girl with her daddy's whole face, she reaches for her, and I allow her to hold her. She joins hands with me, and we walk out of the church together.

I was certain that she was going to show her ass, but she's very polite. A' Meir stands behind me at the burial, making sure that his presence is known. Janet looks at me while they release the doves and says, "He's the one for you. I know that now. If you haven't read your letter yet, you should."

I look at her and begin to cry all over again. We haven't even put the dirt on her son, and now she is okay with me moving on? This has got to be the twilight zone.

CHAPTER NINETEEN

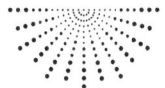

"**Y**ou got it baby girl, come on. Come to mommy," I say as we all wait for Mina to take some steps towards me. She lifts her little foot to come to me, and I get so excited. She stumbles a little but maintains her balance. It isn't until A'Meir steps in front of me that she actually takes more steps.

"Ugh you get on my nerves. Of course she comes to you." I push him out of the way. "What can I say? She loves me, just like her mama."

I look at him and roll my eyes. "That little girl loves you more than I do."

He chuckles as he walks over to me. "Don't be jealous. I love you, too. Ain't that right, Mina? Say 'Daddy loves you too, Mommy.'"

Things have been going smooth these past few months. It seems like after we buried Giavonni, my life fell into place. A'Meir has just been asked to run for mayor, my foundation is partnering with Nike to provide scholarships to local youth that want to better themselves through athletics, and I'm finally happily engaged. At first, I thought his proposal was too soon, but then I realized that the only person holding me back from my future was me. We fell into a routine that provided the most normalcy that I'd had in a long time.

After the funeral, I was tasked with liquidating Giavonni's assets. I reached out to Sincere, and we set up a foundation in Kimber's honor for battered women. We also donated $2.5 million to Kimber's alma mater Spellman college where they now have a garden memorial area set up in her honor.

Sincere didn't want any of G's money for his son that he named Sincere, Jr. He decided that it would be best if his son didn't know how his existence came to be for now. I set up a trust for Mina and deposited $325 million. The remaining $200 million I gave to Janet because I knew that G would have wanted her to be taken care of. She was moved to tears when I presented her with the check last week.

"Did you read your letter yet?" she asked while I stood on her porch.

"No, I've just been so busy that I haven't been able to."

She smiled at me with the same dimples that Giavonni and now Mina had. "When life slows down some, make sure you read it. I think you need to read it sooner than later."

I was curious at her words, but I still managed to brush it off.

Arriving home I find A'Meir and Mina in the driveway preparing to go for a walk. Everyday after we get home he takes Mina for a walk on her push bike around the neighborhood. I kissed them both before going into the house. Even though we had house-keepers I still like to clean my house in between visits, so today I decide to clean my room a little. Mina has been teething, so my bedroom was messier than usual, being that she is the most restless at night. When I move my side table, I find the letter that was given to me by the police seven months ago. I sit on my bed and stare at it for a good ten minutes before opening it. I finally pick the letter up to read it.

Dear Mia,
I hope this letter finds you well. It's crazy. I never thought that I would be writing you a letter

from a jail cell. I have so much that I want to say to you, so I will start from the top. I want to say that I am sorry. The shit that I put you through was not a reflection of the person that you are, it's just a reflection of the man that I was afraid to become. You are an amazing woman, and you didn't deserve any of what I put you through. The lying, the cheating, and partying was me fighting to stay in my youth. I'm sorry for making you feel like it was you. I didn't mean to hurt you the way that I did. Putting my hands on you was never something that I have been able to forgive myself for.

I'm sorry for what I did to our son. I know that you hated me for a while because of what I did. I wanted to take the planning off your plate because I didn't want you to have to do anything but rest. I went back to the hospital when his ashes came in and they said that you and our daughter were gone. I had to ask around just to find out her name. I love the name Mina Joy. She is going to be a princess just like her mommy. I'm sorry that you had to go through the birth alone. I know I acted like an ass, and I am sorry. My last name was all I had to give you, but I was afraid that you were not going to name her after me.

I'm sorry about Kimber. I know that all of this shit is my fault. If I had never been sleeping with her, we would be in bliss. I thought that you were really messing with her husband, but when she told me she was pregnant, I panicked. That is why I said she messaged me. She got in my head, and I started to believe her. Her showing me pictures of you two in Vegas is what made me believe it. The day that she was shot, she came to the house, starting an argument with me, and I left the room to call security, and when I came back, she was gone. It wasn't until after she was shot that I realized that she took our son's ashes. I have lied in the past, but I swear on my soul that I didn't do anything to Kimber.

Sincere came to see me last week. He told me that he knows that I didn't kill his wife. He told me that he was the one who had her killed because she was going to fuck up his namesake having another man's baby. I know that you probably won't believe me, but whatever you do, please make sure that you stay away from Sincere. Kimber told me how obsessed he was with you. How he used to stare at your social media page until he fell asleep. When she would confront him about it, he would beat her. He is not a good guy, Mia, so please stay away. When I told him everything that I knew, he promised me that I would be dead before the end of the trial. I know what I have to do in order to keep you and Mina safe. Please don't be mad at me.

Mayor Frasier also came to see me under the cover of darkness. He told me that he knew I didn't kill Kimber, but it would be impossible for me to beat. He told me that you are dating his son and that you will be protected. I need you to know that it is okay to love him. His dad told me his story, and he is a good man. He is the type of man that I wish I could have been for you. Please don't punish him for my fuck ups. You deserve happiness, and I know he will give that to you and Mina. I want you to consider giving Mina his last name. Don't let her be tied to this mess. I love her just like I love you, and I don't want this world to crucify her for my mistakes.

I love you with all of the heart that I have to give, Mia, and let my baby girl know that I love her. Don't ever doubt if I love you because I do. Please forgive me for what I must do. In my mind, you are already free, now let your heart follow. Because you deserve a love just for Mia.

Love Always.

Giavonni Wallace

. . .

The End

ACKNOWLEDGMENTS

I want to thank my village. There have been many tears, laughs, and times of frustration. To my children Eli, QT, and Nova I love you so much and I thank you for being the light of my life. To my husband Terrence. I thank you for being the love of my life.

Each book I write is shared with a different set of friends, God continues to surround me with people that make me better I say thank you for being my sounding board.

LeCheryl

Leah

Mariah

Ericka

Martina

Bayle

To all my family that continues to support me and allows me to vent even when you have no idea what I am talking about I appreciate it.

Mama Lynne

Bridgette

Aunt Freddie

Uncle Mickey

Denecia

Finally I want to thank me for never giving up and allowing God to guide my pen and help make me better.

ABOUT THE AUTHOR

L. Osborne has always had a love for reading and storytelling. She has always had an active imagination and decided to jump back into the world of writing in late 2023. Growing up in South Carolina, she developed a love for reading and writing in the 3rd grade. As time went on, she became a mother, wife, and entrepreneur which took up many years of her life, but after rediscovering her love for reading in April of 2023 she had an idea that sparked the writer's side of life. She released her debut novella Jonesing For Love: Marina's Motif in July of 2024. Now she has the writing bug and has many stories she is ready to share with the world. Follow her now